ROAD TO MATCHMAKER

a matchmaker mysteries series prequel

elise sax

Manton Public Library
404 West Main Box F
Manton, MI 49663-0906
(231) 824-3584

Road to Matchmaker (A Matchmaker Mysteries Prequel) is a work of fiction. Names, characters, places, and incidents are the products of the author's imagination or are used fictitiously. Any resemblance to actual events, locales, or persons, living or dead, is entirely coincidental.

Copyright © 2017 by Elise Sax
All rights reserved.
ISBN: 978-1978443297
Published in the United States by Elise Sax

Cover design: Elizabeth Mackey
Edited by: NovelNeeds.com and Lynn Mullan
Formatted by: Jesse Kimmel-Freeman

Printed in the United States of America

elisesax.com
elisesax@gmail.com
http://elisesax.com/mailing-list.php
https://www.facebook.com/ei.sax.9
@theelisesax

For Sam, my dreamer.

ALSO BY ELISE SAX

Five Wishes Series
Going Down
Man Candy
Hot Wired
Just Sacked
Wicked Ride
Five Wishes Series

Three More Wishes Series
Blown Away
Inn & Out
Quick Bang

Matchmaker Mysteries Series
Road to Matchmaker
An Affair to Dismember
Citizen Pain
The Wizards of Saws
Field of Screams
From Fear to Eternity
West Side Gory
Scareplane
It Happened One Fright

Operation Billionaire
How to Marry a Billionaire
How to Marry Another Billionaire

Forever Series
Forever Now

Bounty
Switched
Moving Violations

CHAPTER 1..1
CHAPTER 2..14
CHAPTER 3..28
CHAPTER 4..47
CHAPTER 5..59
CHAPTER 6..85
ABOUT THE AUTHOR..99

CHAPTER 1

I was a dreamer. At least that's what I told people. But I was called other things: Lost. Directionless. No rudder.

But I had a rudder. A big, fat rudder that turned me in all kinds of direction all the time. Over and over and over.

That's what happens to dreamers. They dream a never-ending stream of dreams, making them crazy and pulling them this way and that, like a scary, life-altering taffy machine.

My taffy machine had brought me to Los Angeles in April. I had managed to get three jobs so far, but none of them had worked out. That led me to job number four. The good news about job number four was that it came with a wardrobe.

"I don't think it fits," I told my supervisor, Homer. I was wearing a white jumpsuit, which was way too big for me. I had cuffed the legs and the sleeves, but I was still swimming in it. The back of me looked like my butt was drooping to my calves.

"It don't matter," Homer said, digging at the dirt under his fingernails with a flat-head screwdriver. It wasn't working. The dirt was holding strong. "Ain't nobody gonna see you in there."

He shrugged in the direction of a cement truck. There were at least twenty cement trucks in a makeshift parking lot behind the City of Angels Cement For You headquarters building.

"I've never done this before," I said, not wanting to do it.

"You're small, and you know how to hold a hose. That's about all you need."

I was small. I knew how to hold a hose. That was just about the extent of my skills and talents. It had come down to this. I was now a cement truck cleaner. The inside of cement trucks, that is. They used a truck wash machine to clean the outside.

Homer opened the back of the cement truck, revealing a small, circular opening. "I'll heave ho you in there, Gladys. Then, I'll hand you the hose. Here's a scrub brush."

He handed me a large, wire brush, and I tucked it into a pocket of my uniform. Homer interlaced his fingers and leaned over. I put my foot on his hands, and he heave-hoed me. I grabbed onto the rim of the truck's opening and slipped through, crashing down the other side into the belly of the beast.

As I rolled to a stop, my white jumpsuit turned gray with a coat of cement. "I'm in!" I announced.

"Yeah, I know. Here's the hose. I'll be back in a couple of hours," Homer said, slipping the hose into the truck and spraying me with water. After a struggle, I caught the hose and aimed it at the interior walls. The water didn't do much, so I hung it out the opening, and went at the truck with the wire brush. It didn't do much, either. The job required a lot of elbow grease, more than my elbow had. Nevertheless, I scrubbed with every ounce of energy I had because my rent was due, and I had thirty-three dollars in my checking account.

Twenty minutes in, my neck seized up from constantly bending over in the cramped space. It was lucky I wasn't claustrophobic, or I would have been freaking out. My right arm was sore, and I was sweating buckets.

Twenty-two minutes in, my psyche realized that I was stuck in a cement truck with my supervisor gone for hours or maybe forever. The walls of the cement truck seemed to close in on me and my baggy jumpsuit. I clutched onto my wire brush for security. Holy crap. Why did I take a job cleaning out cement trucks? How could I be this stupid?

Actually, I didn't have much choice. My temp agency was running low on possible jobs for me. I was their best client, but their worst worker. I didn't have a lot of staying power, and I either got fired or I quit pretty regularly. I blamed it on my dreaming. The temp jobs never jived with my dreams. I had just worked for two days as the official shower drain cleaner for Los Angeles Real Men Gym, which I thought was pretty long, considering that Real Men had a lot of hair. It never dawned on me that the next job would be even worse.

The truck seemed to get smaller, and my breathing became shallower. I had made barely any progress in the cleaning. Why

3

were cement trucks so small? Why was cement so hard to clean? Why didn't I marry rich or rob a bank instead of a terrible string of temp jobs?

I ducked my head out of the truck's opening. "Hello? Hello?"

Nothing. Not a sound except for the normal cement truck parking lot activity. Nobody came to see who was yelling from inside a cement truck. Taking a deep breath, I tried to calm myself. As soon as I finished cleaning the truck, I would be able to get free.

But then I would have to do another truck.

It was times like these that I wished I had finished high school and had gone on to college. But I wasn't exactly the commitment type, especially commitment to geometry and world history. And I didn't like to be yelled at by teachers and only peeing when I was given a bathroom pass.

Bathroom pass.

Peeing.

"Hello? I need to take a break?" I said like a question. There was still no reply. I dropped the hose out of the truck and let it fall to the ground. Putting the wire brush in my pocket, I carefully slipped through the hole to my freedom.

The air was so much better on the outside of the truck than it was on the inside of the truck. I was covered in cement, which stuck to my body in sweaty clumps. The once-white jumpsuit was gray and wet from the hose and my sweat. My body was like a limp noodle, except for my right arm, which was cramped from the effort.

Working sucked. If I had an extra dollar, I was going to buy a scratch-off lottery ticket on my way home.

"Homer?" I called.

He was still gone. I figured he wouldn't mind if I took a bathroom break. Actually, I wanted to take a forever break. Turning off the hose, I walked across the parking lot into the warehouse. The cement company had a nice breakroom, but nobody else was in it. There was complimentary cereal and milk. I ate only organic, vegan, and I was a diehard fitness buff. Surprisingly, I found a box of Paleo muesli and almond milk. I filled a bowl and dug in.

Not bad. Perhaps I had pre-judged the cement industry. There was even air conditioning.

After the cereal, I turned on the television just in time to catch an episode of *The View*. I almost felt human, again.

"What the devil is going on?" Homer growled, storming into the breakroom. "What're you doing?

"Oh, hi. I was wondering where you were."

"You were what? I thought you had gotten killed. You left the truck without finishing. It looks like you didn't even start."

"I needed a break," I said, as Whoopi said something funny on TV.

Homer's face turned red, and his mouth dropped open. "You couldn't have been in there for more than ten minutes."

"Twenty-one minutes. Boy, it was hot in there. My arm is killing me, too," I said, rubbing my arm, as if to prove my point.

"You...wha...huh...excuse me?" Homer stuttered. Then, he settled on one train of thought. "You're fired!"

I turned off the television. "No! Please! I need this job!"

What was I saying? Being fired was the best possible outcome. I didn't want to go back into the cement truck. I would have rather had my eye poked out with a giant spider leg.

"Please let me get back to work. I swear I won't let you down. I'll do double the amount of trucks you want. Double!" I continued, my mouth betraying me. I didn't know what I was saying. It was like I was high on battery acid or something.

Maybe it was a reaction to cement.

I had found a great apartment in Los Angeles over a small Italian restaurant on a corner in a dilapidated downtown neighborhood. The area had evaded the gentrification of the rest of downtown. I accessed the apartment through a staircase in the back of the restaurant. So, I had to walk past the tables of diners to get home, and I tried to time my comings and goings away from mealtimes. But tonight, I came home at six on the dot, and the restaurant was bursting with people, enjoying spaghetti and veal parmigiana.

Jordan, one of the waiters, was standing outside on the corner, getting some air. His jaw dropped when he saw me get out of my car.

"What happened to you? Are you okay?"

I locked my ancient Oldsmobile and hobbled toward him. "New job."

"Whoa," he said, eyeing me. "What's that in your hair?"

"Cement. I cleaned the inside of six cement trucks."

"Is that a social media joke? I'm not on Facebook."

"No, it's my life. My life is cement trucks."

Jordan nodded, thoughtfully. He was an attractive man, about my age. He was about six-feet-tall with thick, wavy brown hair and big, thoughtful brown eyes. He was wearing a waiter's uniform with a long, black apron.

"I thought you worked at a gym."

"That was two days ago. Today was cement trucks, but they fired me."

Thank God. I should have let Homer fire me when I had only been twenty-one minutes into the first truck, but I had to show him that I could do it. I didn't want to be a failure, again. I wanted to succeed at something. So, I continued cleaning cement trucks. So, six trucks later, he fired me.

Because I couldn't do it. I sucked at cement trucks.

Go figure.

"Sorry to hear that."

Jordan had worked at the restaurant for the past two years while he studied to become a CPA, but he didn't strike me as a numbers guy.

"You want to come in? I'm working on a fettuccine recipe with white truffles."

"I thought you were a waiter, Jordan."

He looked around, as if he expected someone to jump out between the buildings. "I am, but sometimes, I...cook. But I'm going to be a CPA."

He added the last part, like he was trying to convince himself.

"It sounds delicious, but I'm a vegan."

Jordan's face dropped, which was a common reaction to my strict dietary habits. I hadn't eaten junk food in years, and I was an obsessive spin class junkie. But I didn't know how I was going to get up the next morning and move my body. My right arm was pinned to my side, too painful to move.

I heard a whimper. At first, I thought it might be me, but it turned out to be a dog. It stepped out of the doorway, next door, took a couple steps and whimpered, again.

"Look at that dog," I said. "What's he doing?"

"That's Ralph. He doesn't want to get electrocuted. His owner strung an electric wire so the dog couldn't run away."

"That's not very nice," I commented. I had a strong desire to free the dog and let it run wild through the streets of downtown, even though that wouldn't be wise. "Can we turn off the electricity?"

"I don't think the owner would like that, and he's sort of ornery. Besides, the dog knows not to touch the wire, so he isn't in any danger."

"I'm sorry," I called to the dog. He whimpered again and went back to his place in the doorway. I wanted to find my place, too. I was worn out. "I better get in and take a shower," I told Jordan.

He opened the door to the restaurant for me. "It was nice seeing you."

I walked upstairs and unlocked my apartment. I had never been so happy to see a tiny studio with furniture from the 1970s. I peeled off my shirt just as the phone rang. Digging it out of my purse, I answered. It was my grandmother, who lived in a small town in the mountains, east of San Diego. I hadn't seen her for about five years, but she was my closest family member. I only had two, my mother and my grandmother. I hadn't seen my mother since the last time she asked for money, which was like asking the Gobi Desert for a house on the lake.

"Hello, bubbeleh," my grandmother said. "This is your

yearly, happy birthday call. Are you ready?" She started to sing happy birthday to me before I had a chance to answer. I had completely forgotten it was my birthday. April thirteenth. One more year. How could I have forgotten? It might have been because I didn't want to think about getting older while crammed in the belly of a cement truck.

"Thank you, Grandma," I said when she finished singing.

"Dolly, I'm going to tell you something."

Grandma was the center of her town and a renowned matchmaker. She pretty much told people things from morning until night. She also had a way of knowing things that couldn't be known. Yes, she was wise, but it was more than that. She had a wickedly talented sixth sense. A third eye. So, it was always good to listen to her, even if I didn't want to.

"Okay, Grandma. Shoot."

"You're a good person, but if you want to grow and change, you can go ahead and do that. Evolve. It's your time, bubbeleh. Your time to move on."

"All I do is move on, Grandma. I've lived in six different cities since the beginning of the year. I think I'm going for the world record for the most jobs in a lifetime. I get fired faster than Superman can change to save Lois Lane."

"That's fast."

"Today I got fired, again."

"I know. At least the cement truck didn't blow up," Grandma said, somehow knowing about the humiliation that preceded my termination from the cement company.

"I didn't mean to set it on fire," I told her. "I was just checking my work, and it was getting dark."

"And you didn't have a flashlight, but you had a book of matches in your pocket," my grandmother finished for me.

"It wasn't even my pocket, so it wasn't my fault that there were matches in there."

"Homer's hair will grow back," Grandma told me, comfortingly. My boss had appeared just as the fireball started. I was never going to forget the look on poor Homer's face the moment he realized that a fireball was coming right for him from the back of the cement truck.

Somehow, I didn't get burned. Not even a burned finger. The fire seemed to have a mind of its own and just like I wanted to, ran out of the truck as fast as it could. *Poof!* It hit Homer and took his hair with it.

"How about his eyebrows?" I asked my grandmother.

"Nope. Those will be gone forever. But he's not hurt."

Phew. "That's good. The paramedics hinted that it was my fault."

There was a long pause. I guessed she wanted to say something diplomatic but was at a loss for words. She was right, and so were the paramedics. It was totally my fault that Homer would never arch an eyebrow again.

"You have a gift, Dolly, but it's not for cement trucks," she said, finally.

I wanted to ask her what my gift was, but I was afraid to ask. What if it was for something worse than cement trucks? Actually, after a lifetime of failed temporary jobs, I doubted I had any gifts. I was giftless. I was a bad Christmas or a bad birthday.

Speaking of bad birthdays, I looked at the small pile of bills on my kitchen table for a birthday card that I might have missed. Sure enough, there was a card from my grandmother. I opened it, and a check for twenty-five dollars fell out.

"Thank you for the card, Grandma."

"My pleasure. Remember what I said. You have a gift. A calling. You're going to move on. It'll be like you're someone else. Don't be scared."

Then, she hung up. I had no idea what she meant, but I was sort of bummed to have been reminded that it was my birthday. The day had evolved from a miserable day to a miserable and supremely disappointing day.

Usually, I ate and got drunk on my birthday, but this one was a reminder that my life was no place. No friends were calling me. I didn't have a party or a gluten-free, vegan cake.

I stripped down and walked into the bathroom. Turning on the shower, I got in and started to scrub the cement off me. My hair was thick with it, and it reminded me that I felt guilty about

Homer's now-bald head.

After finally getting clean, I turned off the water. But before I could open the shower curtain, a large hand reached in and grabbed me hard. I struggled against the grip, but I wasn't strong enough.

I screamed.

CHAPTER 2

Nobody came to save me, which was fine because it turned out that it was only Nat Pendleton who was grabbing me in the shower. I had gone out with him two times, and I didn't want a third date. I had gone through bad men like they were peanut M&Ms. I was a loser magnet. Unfortunately, I had gone out with Nat when I was having a particularly horny moment, so he had already seen me naked.

But I didn't want him to see me naked again. And here he was, standing in my bathroom with the shower curtain pushed aside, one of his hands clutching my arm, and his other hand holding a bouquet of birthday balloons.

He smiled wide. His teeth were blindingly white. Twice as white as his eyeballs. I instantly regretted sleeping with him, even more than I regretted sleeping with him right after I slept with him. There was no attraction to him. None. I was so unattracted to him, that I didn't even cover up my nudity when he surprised me in the bathroom.

"Just me. Just me," he said, still smiling. "No need to scream."

I stopped screaming. "Wha… Huh?" I said.

"Surprise! Happy birthday, baby."

Ugh. Blech. I hated being called "baby." Especially by Nat.

"How did you know it was my birthday?"

"I Googled you, of course. I know everything about you."

I shuddered and wrapped a towel around my nakedness. I wasn't thrilled about the idea of Nat cyberstalking me or breaking into my apartment. I was about to tell him off, pop his balloons, and kick him out on his ass.

"I've come to whisk you away for your birthday dinner," he continued.

My stomach growled, betraying me. I was starving. I hadn't eaten since my bowl of Paleo muesli. I didn't want to eat with Nat, but I was now unemployed, it was my birthday, and a free meal was a free meal.

"Okay. Get out, and I'll get dressed," I said without a hint of excitement in my voice. Nat kissed my closed lips and skipped out of the bathroom.

I got dressed in jeans and a sweater and tied back my wet hair. I skipped the makeup and the perfume because I didn't want to encourage him.

"All righty," I said, picking up my purse. "I'm ready."

"You look nice," he said. I guessed I wasn't the only horny person in Los Angeles. Nat looked like he wanted to get down to business, but he had the good graces to feed me first. "You'll love where we're going to eat."

He wanted to surprise me, but it didn't take long for me to find out where we were going. It turned out that Nat had reserved a corner table downstairs in the Italian restaurant under my apartment. Jordan was our waiter.

"Back for that fettuccini with white truffles?" Jordan asked.

"Not this time, Jordan. I'm sorry. I'll have a salad." The biggest struggle in being healthy and maintaining my health was good, old-fashioned peer pressure. It was like a global conspiracy to make me fat. But no way was I going to gain weight. I was never going to bow to the pressure to eat crap. I was in perfect shape, and I wasn't going to go off track. Besides, I couldn't afford new clothes.

Nat ordered lasagna, making Jordan's face drop. But half of the restaurant was enjoying his creation. Even though Jordan was a waiter, his food was a big hit. I wondered why he wanted to be a CPA when he had obvious talents as a cook. I didn't have talents as a cook. I had worked in a Cheesecake Factory kitchen for two hours, so I knew. It didn't end well. Cops were called.

Jordan left to put in our order, and Nat leaned forward with his elbows on the table and his fingers interlaced with his chin resting on them. He had hair growing out of his left nostril, and I wondered why I had slept with him. He wasn't the first man with hair sticking out of his nose that I had hit the sheets with, but I hoped to hell he was the last. I had been on a bad run with bad men for the past five years or so, and I was getting tired of them. My vagina was going to rebel at any moment. It was probably going to fall out and run for the hills if it saw one more man like Nat.

Actually, that would solve a lot of problems. Men problems. Goodbye, vagina. It was nice knowing you. You did everything you were supposed to, and I let you down with loser men and plain soap instead of fancy vaginal wash.

With all of my deep thoughts about my vagina, I hadn't realized that Nat had been talking to me. "Huh?" I asked.

"Later, after our dinner. Not leather restraints. Just silk scarves. You can trust me. We can give you a safe word. Not, 'ouch.' You'll be saying that a lot. How about, 'hot stuff?'"

My eyes teared, and I realized that I wasn't blinking.

"Uh…" I said. "what did you say?"

"S and M. Fifty Shades action. Bondage. Time to move this thing we got up a few notches. Raise the roof. Increase the decibels. Doesn't that sound good? I knew from the first moment I saw you that you would submit to me. Total submission. Like a golden retriever."

He moved his eyebrows up and down. Ironically, Jordan arrived with the food just then, at the very moment when I had completely lost my appetite.

"Here you go. Would you like anything else?" Jordan asked. "Fresh ground pepper? Parmesan?"

I wanted to leave, to return to my apartment, watch TV, and fall asleep. I wanted to knee Nat in the balls and wash my vagina out with bleach. Blech. I was done with men. Men and me didn't mix.

I was about to ask Jordan to give me a box for my salad to go and to tell Nat goodbye, when a very thin woman walked into the restaurant and stopped near our table. She was all angles and pointy parts, her cheeks sticking out like they were trying to escape her severe face. Where I wasn't wearing any makeup, she had painted her face with a large brush. Her lips had a purple outline and bright red interior, and her eyelids were black, rimmed with long, fake eyelashes. Keeping with the theme, her shoes were pointy and so was her purse. She was wearing a tight suit with a blue miniskirt.

For a panic-filled moment, I thought that Nat had invited her to join us in his planned night of kinky debauchery, but she ignored us completely. Instead, she pointed her pointy nose right at our waiter, Jordan. She hooked her pointy finger at him, and he walked to her.

"Don't forget you have to see your advisor tomorrow and talk to him about your classes. I'm not sure accounting 206 is what you should do right now," she told Jordan.

He was like a deer caught in the headlights, and I got the

impression that it was a regular thing for him. Poor deer. Even though he was a head taller than the pointy woman, he seemed to shrink down and look up at her in fear. "Yes, dear," he said.

"Don't work late. Remember to keep the eye on the prize. CPA. That's your goal."

"Yes, dear."

"This is not real, you know. You can't hang a life on pasta."

"Yes, dear."

"Remember that we're going to buy a house in Bel Air in two years. Two years, Jordan."

"Yes, dear."

"A house in Bel Air is a lot of pasta. You realize that, right?"

"Yes, dear."

"On second thought, I wouldn't mind some Parmesan," Nat called, interrupting Jordan's conversation.

Jordan blinked and did a little hop, obviously distressed that he had let a diner down. "Right away," he said.

While he jogged to the kitchen, the pointy woman crossed her arms in front of her and stared down at our plates. I took a self-conscious bite of my salad, keeping one eye on the pointy woman. The salad was delicious, but it was hard to focus on it when I had

Nat and the pointy woman staring at me. Nat, in particular, was disconcerting. He kept winking at me, and smiling with half of his mouth, and I could practically see the images of my naked body in bondage playing in his brain like an old-fashioned porno playing in a dirty movie theater. Gross.

Jordan returned and grated Parmesan onto Nat's food. "Anything else I can do for you?"

I felt a surge of protectiveness over Jordan, and I decided to butt in to defend him against a woman who wanted to chain him to a calculator for the rest of his life.

"We're fine," I said. "Jordan, the whole restaurant is enjoying your truffle pasta. You must be very proud. You're a natural talent. You'll be a great chef someday." I said the last bit while locking eyes with the pointy woman.

Bully. She was a pointy, well-dressed bully. I hated bullies, probably because all forms of injustice got under my skin. Most people just tweeted about injustice, but I fumed and obsessed about injustice. I wanted a fair deal for every Tom, Dick, and Jordan.

Poor Jordan wasn't getting a fair deal. He had a gift for pasta, but he was being railroaded into doing math. I hated math.

"Hey Jordan, I changed my mind," I told him. "I would love some of your pasta."

His face brightened, but he shot a scared look at the woman. He swallowed visibly. "I'll get you a plate," he told me with a smile.

This time, the pointy woman followed him to the kitchen. I could hear her harangue him about focusing on self-employment tax as they walked. Nat leaned forward again and took my hand. "So…" he started.

I pulled my hand back. "I'm not going to have sex with you, Nat. Never again. No more naked."

"We could do it without getting naked," he said, reasonably.

He was right. We could do it without getting naked. Then, I wouldn't have to touch him…ish.

No. What the hell was I thinking? I was done with losers. I was done with men who made me want to clean my vagina out with Clorox after I slept with them. Done. Done. Done. I was going to be a nun.

Oh! That was a great idea.

"I'm going to be a nun," I told Nat.

"I thought you were Jewish."

I looked up at the ceiling, as if an answer would fall from the stucco. "It's a new branch of nuns," I said, finally. "It's like regular nuns, but light on Jesus and heavy on guilt."

"I like nuns," he said, but thankfully, he didn't sound entirely certain. "Well," he said, looking down at his food.

Jordan returned with the pasta that I didn't really want, and the pointy woman sat at the bar. I had hoped she would leave

Manton Public Library
404 West Main Box F
Manton, MI 49663-0906
(231) 824-3584

so I didn't have to eat the pasta, but now I would have to eat every last drop and gain five pounds.

Jordan hovered over me while I took the first bite. "Holy shit, that's the best thing I've ever had in my mouth," I moaned.

Nat must have taken that as an insult to him because he muttered under his breath, "Just gets better and better."

We ate in complete silence. Nat had given up, thank goodness. He didn't even look at my boobs again, even though they looked fabulous in the sweater I was wearing. I ate every drop of Jordan's pasta. It was delicious. I could feel the cellulite breaking out on my ass as I chewed, but a little voice deep inside me told me that it was worth it. Besides, I was now a nun, so who cared about a little cellulite?

After our pasta, Jordan suggested dessert, but Nat refused, even though it was my birthday, which didn't upset me because I had already eaten enough carbs for the next week. But then there was the little issue of the bill.

"I think we should split this," he said.

Since I had twenty-five dollars to my name, he would've had to split the bill into tiny little pieces. "This is my birthday dinner. You invited me."

"Listen, Gladie. I would never have invited you to dinner if I knew you were going to become a nun."

He had a point. "What's your point? You only buy dinner for women if you know you're going to get some afterword?"

"Duh! I could've taken out at least five other women, you know. Or I could've sat home, eating takeout and watching the basketball game on TV."

"So you treat women like whores."

"I don't buy whores dinner."

We went back-and-forth for a while, but in the end, I won, because you can't get blood out of a stone or $22.50 from a woman who couldn't hold down a cement truck cleaning job. Nat tipped Jordan ten percent and stormed out of the restaurant. I would have felt embarrassed, but the ball of pasta digesting in my stomach had a tranquilizing effect on me that was kind of like a good buzz.

I stood up. It was time to go back upstairs and watch *Murder She Wrote* reruns, but I liked the ambiance in the small restaurant. People were happy, eating their carbs, and if anyone's dates was suggesting bondage as a post-meal activity, nobody seemed upset by it. The servers seemed pretty happy, too, all except for Jordan who was being told off by his girlfriend at the bar.

It dawned on me that if I worked there, I would have a four-second commute. And probably a free meal every day. My brain whirred into action. I went to the bar and leaned against it, as if I was cool and wasn't about to beg for a job.

"Hey, Jordan," I said, smiling professionally. "Excuse me," I added to the pointy lady because I had interrupted her monologue about the importance of summer school so that Jordan would get his CPA license faster. "I was wondering if there were any job openings here, and if you could put a good word in for me."

"Sure, I would put a good word in for you," he said. "But we just hired someone, so there's no openings." My face must have dropped because Jordan leaned forward. "But I'll drop your name the first time there's an opening."

"If you're still here, Jordan," the pointy woman said. "Jordan's going to be a CPA," she told me.

"Yes, dear," Jordan said, probably out of habit.

I couldn't stand the pointy woman. She was a bully, and she was turning Jordan into a miniature person. I was about to let her have it. It was the only way to deal with bullies. Be tough with them and take them down to size. I was ready to put her in her place and prevent her from ever making Jordan say, "yes, dear," again.

"If you're looking for a job, I might know of one for you," the pointy woman told me.

Oh. Perhaps I had been hasty in my judgment of her. She didn't seem so bad.

"Really?"

She took her phone out of her purse and tapped it. "I know someone with a used bookstore, and she's looking for someone to do inventory. Do you like books?"

I didn't *not* like books. I wasn't a big reader, but a used bookstore sounded like heaven after my day of cement trucks. "I love books," I gushed at my newfound hero. "I like nothing more than reading."

Yes, I was a liar. Yes, I was a hypocrite. Yes, I was morally bankrupt, sucking up to the pointy woman because she held the promise of a job inventorying books. The truth was that I hadn't read a book since I had stumbled on my mother's copy of *The Valley of the Dolls* when I was fourteen. Sure, I had read a Grisham or two, but in school, I was strictly *Cliff Notes* all the way. All the way until I dropped out.

"Give me your name," she commanded.

"Gladie Burger."

"What kind of name is that? Sounds made up."

"Uh…"

But she didn't wait for an answer. "Okay. I texted Francine. Be there at ten tomorrow morning. Corner of Black and Rose Avenues. Got it?"

No. I had no idea where that was, but I would find it. "Yes. Thank you so much."

Just like that, I had a new job. It was like a miracle, and a pointy woman with a fetish for accountants was my Moses. Go figure.

No matter how many jobs I got, I was always imbued with a sense of optimism whenever I got hired. It was a fresh start. The possibilities were endless. Each job could lead to wonderful things, like my soulmate of work. A lifetime of fulfillment and joy. It could have happened. It was possible. Julia Child had seemed happy with her job. Ditto Wyatt Earp. There were people who had jobs that they called "callings," and they did them for their whole lives, and they couldn't wait to get to work every morning. So, here I was again, fantasizing that doing inventory in a used bookstore was my calling.

I was excited.

I was so pleased about that job that I knew I wouldn't be able to get to sleep yet. So, instead of climbing the stairs to my apartment, I walked through the restaurant and outside to breathe in the night air. The pointy woman was leaving at the same time, and Jordan walked her out. I said, thank you to her, again, almost calling her pointy woman because I had never gotten her real name.

Jordan kissed her goodbye with a peck on her closed mouth. "Don't stay late," she commanded as she left.

"Yes, dear," he told her back as she walked away.

Instead of fresh, night air, there was a cloud of cigarette smoke, and it was coming from one cigarette. I recognized the outline of Nat in the shadows, and a small light by his face when he took a drag.

"Coming back to beg me for a second chance?" Nat sneered at me. He dropped his cigarette and crushed it under his shoe.

I froze and didn't say a word. I hated conflict of any kind. I didn't want to fight with Nat. I wanted to run inside and hide in my apartment, but Jordan was behind me, and I didn't want to look like a chicken, either.

"No second chances, baby," Nat said, his voice rising an octave. He was being extremely aggressive, but he was backing up as he did it. "There's plenty of beauties lining up for a piece of Nat. Believe you me!" The street light flickered, which gave the illusion that he was moving backward without actually walking. It also made it seem like the dog from before appeared as if by magic. The dog had probably come out to see what the yelling was about. Nat continued to back up. "You ate two entrees, and what do I get? Nothing. Well, you get nothing, too, sweet cheeks. And you're going to be begging me later. You bitch."

"Hey, now," Jordan said raising his hand up, like he was hailing a taxi. "No need for that kind of talk. There's a lady here. Uh oh. Mister, you should probably stop backing up."

"I'm not scared of you," Nat spat at Jordan.

But he should have listened to him because Jordan was right. Nat should have stopped backing up, but he was so focused on his lack of nookie that he didn't realize he was heading for the electric fencing that kept the dog in place. I didn't realize it either until he suddenly stopped talking, his body went stiff, and he shouted, "I'm hot!" and collapsed dead away.

CHAPTER 3

I never found out if Nat had screamed, "I'm hot!" because he was announcing his attractiveness in the face of my rejection or if electric shock made him warm. In any case, Nat recovered pretty quickly, but Jordan insisted on calling the paramedics to check him out, who in turn called the ASPCA for the dog, who was taken away. Later, I found out that the dog had found a forever home with a hipster, Extreme Frisbee player.

I stayed out of the whole incident because Nat held onto a grudge with a death grip. While I watched as the paramedics took care of him, he continued to rail against women—especially me—who were ungrateful for free meals, which included two entrees. Finally, they took him away, and I went to bed.

The next morning, I dressed for doing inventory in a used bookstore, which in my case was a short, green skirt and a white blouse. As I drove to the bookstore, I got a case of the butterflies. It wasn't a secret that I had been fired from about a thousand jobs. I had yet to find a boss who thought I was a natural and appreciated my work ethic.

Sure, I probably didn't have a work ethic, but that fact didn't stop me from trying to find one. I guessed I was getting burned out from going from one job to another. And getting fired.

My new job turned out to be one of the easiest I had ever had, but my new boss Francine had learned her leadership skills from De Sade and Attila the Hun. She looked like she could have been the pointy woman's twin, but with a long, pointy nose, making her look even more pointy.

"Don't think that this will be a walk in the park," she told me in the stacks of used paperbacks. "Because this is hard work. If I see you loafing, I'll fire you and you won't see a penny. You get me?"

"Yes," I said. It wasn't the first time that I had had a scary boss. I was hoping that she was doing the scary thing up front to keep me in line but would settle down once I started organizing books.

"And you're going to have to work fast. Are you ready to work fast?"

"Uh…" I said, slowly.

"It's a mess in here, and I'm sick of it. The romance is mixed with the mystery. Thrillers are mixed with science fiction. It's bedlam. Chaos. I want you to start with romance. That's our biggest seller. Women come in here during their lunch breaks and buy a book every day."

"They read a book every day?" I asked, stunned.

She arched an eyebrow. "You're a big reader, too, right? I need someone who really knows commercial fiction."

"I'm a huge reader," I lied. "If I'm not reading Stephen King, I'm totally into Stephenie Meyer." That was it. The extent of my knowledge about authors. *The Shining* and *Twilight*, and I hadn't even read those. I had only watched the movies. My new boss nodded her head very slowly, and her eyes roamed my face, as if she could tell from it how much I actually read. I put on my best librarian face, which entailed a slight smile with no teeth and an amazing ability not to blink. It worked. She nodded and pointed to the bookshelves behind her.

"Start there. You can take an hour lunch at twelve."

And that was it. That was my training. Like a miracle from God, the pointy woman left me totally alone to organize her bookstore. She spent the entire day sitting in a bedazzled chair at the front of the shop next to the cash register, calling friends to complain about the contractor who was renovating her kitchen and playing Candy Crush.

Even though I didn't know a Julia Quinn novel from a Janet Evanovich, it was easy to tell romance from mystery just by looking at the covers. I decided to first remove the mysteries from the romance section and then organize romance before tackling mysteries.

It was a relaxing task. Handling each book, I took a moment to look at the cover and imagine the story. If I continued working there, I could see me becoming a reader. Just as I had been told, at around eleven o'clock, a few women came in and searched the romance shelves for their day's book.

"Where's Susan Mallery?" one woman in a suit and beige pumps asked me.

"I saw some next to Debbie Macomber," I said, pointing to a shelf next to me. I was pretty proud of myself for knowing who Susan Mallery and Debbie Macomber were after one hour of shuffling through books. The job was growing on me. I finally felt like I was getting someplace, that maybe I had found my purpose in life.

Another woman walked in and stepped over me, as I sat on the floor, surrounded by piles of books. She studied the mystery section, her face settling into a scowl.

"Are you kidding me?" she demanded, looking at the rows of books.

"May I help you?" I asked.

"You don't have *Hard to Die*?"

"Hard to…?"

"I read *Hard to Kill* and *Hard to Catch*, and if I don't read the next in the series, I'll kill myself."

"What series is that?"

The woman stared at me like I had sprouted a second head on my shoulders. "The *Harriet Hard* mystery series. You haven't heard of Harriet Hard?"

Once again, I felt like an idiot. Was I supposed to have heard of Harriet Hard? "Well…"

The woman threw her hand over her heart and closed her eyes. "It's the best series I've ever read. I so want to be Harriet Hard. She's a spy catcher. She travels all around the world and has wild adventures. She's totally kickass with a to-die-for wardrobe. *Hard to Catch* ended on a cliffhanger, and I have to get my hands on *Hard to Die*, or I don't know what I'll do. You'll never believe how book two ended."

"How?" I breathed. Her enthusiasm was contagious. Harriet Hard sounded like the kind of woman I wanted to become. And she sounded like she had a steady job, too.

The woman bent her knees slightly and put her hands out, like she was preparing to catch a ball. "Okay. This is what happened. Harriet Hard was locked in a warehouse with a twenty-megaton bomb, and then…"

I was riveted to the story for another five minutes before she had to return to work. I promised her that I would search for *Hard to Die* and hopefully have it for her the next day. I stopped what I was doing and attacked the mystery shelves. It didn't take me long to find five copies of *Hard to Kill*, the first book in the series. I opened up to the first page.

Harriet Hard had picked a rotten day to die. Not only was it her spa day, but it was also her birthday. She was perfectly aware that her assistant,

Ronaldo, had a surprise party waiting for her at Chez Pierre—the swankiest new restaurant in town—for lunch, but now she would have to miss her party, miss lunch, and go through the day with unpolished toenails. All because she was going to die.

Holy crap. It was the best book, ever. I was hooked, immediately. For the first time in my life, I couldn't put a book down. Quickly, I read how Harriet Hard almost died three times but managed to survive through her smarts, good luck, amazing flexibility, and a rocket launcher.

"You can take your lunch break now," my new boss interrupted. "You're not reading a book, are you?"

I slammed the book closed.

"Oh, no, just making sure it's mystery. I'm splitting up romance and mystery first, and then I'm going to organize the romance by author."

She seemed to think about that for a moment. Then, she nodded. "Okay. But remember to do it fast. Take your lunch break now so I can go in an hour."

I ate an apple in my car while I devoured as much of the book as I could during my lunch break. Harriet Hard had escaped again, and now she was in a head-to-head, cerebral battle with her arch nemesis, Hugo Rockchenko, at a fancy restaurant.

Harriet laid her linen napkin on her lap, which was firm and shapely from years of elite combat training. Her sleeveless silk gown was cut low in front, and the man sitting before her let his eyes dip to the place where her breasts met, revealing tantalizing cleavage. But even though the infamous Russian spy and assassin, Hugo Rockchenko, was obviously attracted to Harriet, experience had proved more than once that he would have killed her any chance he got. Poisoning, running her down with a Mack truck, and shooting at her with a high-powered sniper rifle were among the ways that he had already tried to do away with his arch-nemesis, but Harriet Hard was hard to kill. Very hard to kill. The hardest. But he wasn't going to give up. Harriet was sure of that.

So, while they ate their gourmet dinner, Harriet kept a small caliber pistol strapped to her inner thigh, prepared to blow a hole between Rockchenko's eyes with the smallest provocation. Now, however, she was busy eating her caviar on little toast points and sipping her second glass of Don Perignon, all the while listening to what Rockchenko had to offer.

"A truce," he said, his voice dripping with the accent from a fine Russian boarding school.

Harriet laughed, lustily. "Why would I trust you with a truce?"

"Because if you don't, and we can't work together, there will be a world war, and this time it'll mean total devastation. The complete loss of

human life on the planet."

"Nuclear war?" Harriet asked.

"Chemical. A new toxin that melts the face right off a person. Melted faces, Harriet. This thing is bigger than our little spat."

My lunch hour sped by. I didn't want to stop reading. I needed to find out what would happen between Harriet and the Russian spy. I hid the book in my purse when I returned to the bookstore. My boss left right away to go to lunch, and instead of going back to my inventory, I sat among the piles of books and continued to read about Harriet Hard's adventures. Quickly, I got back into the story. Murder! Mayhem! Melted faces! It was a rollercoaster of action and emotion. Then, it took a turn I never saw coming.

With deft fingers, Hugo Rockchenko unhooked Harriet's lacy bra and garters, letting them slip to the floor. His muscular arms encircled her waifish waist and pulled her against him roughly, allowing her to feel the length and breadth of his rigid desire for her. Then, his lips attacked her, possessing her, and in that moment, he went from being Harriet's arch-nemesis to her lover. Forbidden fruit that could get her killed.

Or worse.

"What are you doing? You're reading, aren't you? I can see that you're reading."

"Huh?" I said and then realized that my boss had returned. I had read through her lunch break and hadn't heard her come back. I had a delayed reaction, jumping in fear. I screamed and threw up my hands, throwing the book against a stack of romance and making the other books topple to the floor.

"I wasn't reading," I lied, out of breath.

"This is exactly why I fired the last girl." She wasn't buying it. She knew I was a liar.

"It won't happen again."

She wagged her finger at me. "It better not. I told you I wanted you to work fast. Fast. You can't work fast if you're not working."

She had a point.

"I swear it'll never happen, again," I said, holding up three fingers. "I just...just..." Had to find out what happened with Harriet Hard! And she was about to get naked with Hugo!

"Fine. This is your warning. If it happens again, you'll have to go," she told me and went back to the cash register.

The rest of the day, I tried to work, but every chance I got, I would slip back into the book to read a few pages. It was like resisting chocolate or Chris Pratt.

When the day finally ended, I went home with book one and book two hidden in my purse. I waved to Jordan on my way through the Italian restaurant and took the stairs two at a time to my little apartment. The moment I opened the door, I threw my body onto the couch and opened the book again. I tore through the book and moved onto the second. I read all night and got to the last chapter as the sun began to rise.

> *"One of us is going to die, Harriet, and it's not going to be you," Hugo said, cradling Harriet's face. "Let me throw my body onto the bomb to shield you."*

> *Harriet's eyes filled with tears, a first in years. She didn't want to shed tears for her murderous enemy, but damn it, she couldn't deny what she felt for Hugo.*

> *"No," she pleaded. "Let me try to dismantle the bomb, again. If I remove the timer, then the…"*

> *Hugo put his finger over her lips, quieting her. "My darling, this is the end. We must say goodbye now, or we won't have any time."*

> *The bomb glowed hot, signaling that it was about to explode. The enemies turned lovers didn't have a lot of time.*

> *"I'll find a way to save you, Hugo. If it's the last thing I do!"*

> *He took a step backward and smiled wide.*

> *He smiled like a wolf about to devour its prey.*

"What?" Harriet asked. Her skin broke out in goosebumps, and the hair on the back of her neck stood up. Her sharp instincts returned to her, and she knew that she had been fooled and manipulated by the master spy in front of her.

"You fell for the whole thing, hook, line, and sinker," he said, laughing. "It was the easiest operation I've ever done. Kisses instead of bullets. Who would have thought it would be so simple?"

Harriet's blood boiled. Her pulse raced. She had been played by her arch-enemy. She had let herself be tricked. She had forgotten all of her training and ignored her instincts.

"What's your plan, Rockchenko?" she hissed between her teeth.

"Well, let's see," he said, studying his fingernails. "I have you in a closed space with a bomb, which is ready to explode. I think it's clear. I'm going to kill you and destroy the free world. Say goodbye, Harriet Hard."

Harriet had prevented a nuclear attack three years before. She had protected the president from a kidnapping attempt the year before. And just that week, she had saved a litter of kittens from drowning. She knew deep in her heart that Hugo Rockchenko had her dead to rights, but she also knew that there was no way she would let him get out of *this alive.*

She had to save the free world, and no bomb or super spy was going to stop her.

The fact that she had been fooled would haunt her for the rest of her life, but on the bright side, she would probably only live for another thirty seconds.

"I'll say goodbye," Harriet told Rockchenko. "But I'm taking you with me."

"Don't be foolish. You can't defeat me," he said, but his eyes told a different story. He was scared. Wary.

Smart guy.

The bomb began to beep, which was the signal right before it was going to blow. Her archnemesis slowly made his way to the door. But she wasn't going to let him escape. It was now or never. Harriet had to make her move and save the free world.

And get her revenge on the man who played with her heart.

The End

The end?

The end?

I searched for more pages, but besides a note about the next book in the series and a paragraph about the author, there was nothing. It was the dreaded cliffhanger. How could that bitch author do that to me?

It was the best book I had ever read.

It was even better than the first book in the series, which had been the best book I had ever read until I read the second book in the series.

The story had had everything. Adventure. Sex. International, luxury locales. I was hooked. I needed the next book, pronto, in order to heal myself from the shock of the ending. I had been sure that Hugo was Harriet's soulmate. Her true love. They had been perfect for each other. He was the only man who could equal Harriet in hand-to-hand combat and her ability to read ancient cuneiform texts.

But it had all been a lie. A con. A scam. A betrayal. So typical of men.

Poor Harriet Hard. First the man of her dreams had chewed her up and spit her out, and then she was trapped in a factory with a mega-bomb that was about to blow up. Life was so unfair!

I had to get the next book in the series, immediately. I couldn't survive without knowing what happened to Harriet Hard.

My stomach growled. Reading was great for my diet. I had been so riveted by the stories that I hadn't eaten a thing besides the apple. It was horrible for sleep, though. I hadn't slept a wink all night, and there was no time for a nap before I had to get ready to go to work.

It wasn't until I walked into the bookstore that I remembered that we didn't have the third book, or at least we couldn't find it. I didn't have time or money to get to another bookstore and buy the book, so I rolled up my sleeves and promised myself that I was going to find it if it was the last thing I did.

I became an inventory animal. I ripped through the romance section like Superman dealing with the Penguin or whoever Superman dealt with. In any case, I was a superhero. Amazing.

There was no *Hard to Die* in the romance section, though. On to mystery. I got through half of the stacks when the customer from the day before came in.

"Did you find it? Did you find it?" she asked, breathlessly.

I wiped a few locks of hair off my sweaty cheek with the back of my hand. "No. I've been looking all day, but I'm not giving up."

The woman's eyes grew big, as if she was a cow on its way to the slaughterhouse. "Are you kidding me? I've looked all over this town, and nothing. Barnes and Noble didn't have one copy, either. Amazon has a used copy for thirty-six dollars. I guess I have to get that. You know, the publisher canceled the series after the third book."

"You're kidding," I said. "They're the best books I've ever read. They're better than TV. What am I going to do after the third book?"

I had just started reading, and now I was being kicked in the teeth because of it. Television would have never let me down like this.

"I'm going to buy my used copy before someone gets it before me," the customer announced and made a beeline for the door.

I continued to search through the mystery section. The store had never looked better. I was a mix of Martha Stewart and a person who was really good at organizing books. Every book was dusted and put in its place. I was the inventory champion goddess of the planet. Desperation had turned me into the employee of the century. Of the universe.

"Oh my God," my boss said, surprising me, as I crouched on my hands and knees, searching for the damned book behind the stacks. "Did you do this?"

I sat up. "What? Did I do something wrong?"

"Uh, no. I mean, you're doing an adequate job. Keep it up. But it's closing time."

"It is?" I had never worked beyond my hours before. I normally watched the clock, like a lion watches a gazelle at lunch time. "I spent eight hours nonstop, organizing books?"

"That's what you're supposed to do," she said, looking at the pristine bookshelves.

She had a point. It was my brightest moment in my long and varied work history. But I hadn't found the book yet, and I wasn't ready to quit. I needed to know what happened to Harriet Hard.

"Do you mind if I stay a little longer?" I asked. "I just have a little more I want to finish before I leave. I promise to lock up."

I watched my boss's face as she debated leaving me alone in the store in the evening to do God knew what. But the possibility of having even more beautiful, pristine bookshelves was a strong temptation.

"You don't have to pay me for the extra hours," I added, and her eyes widened, like she was on a really good date with George Clooney.

"Don't forget to lock up after," she said and then she was gone.

I stood in the center of the stacks and turned around, slowly. The book had to be there, somewhere. I scanned every shelf, and miracle of miracle, I spotted about a dozen paperbacks on top of one bookcase, crammed into a corner.

"Oh, please. Oh, please. Oh, please," I muttered, as I climbed up the step ladder. I knew that the chances that the book I was searching for was among a small pile on top of the bookcase were slim to none, but I still held out hope.

I stretched my hand out and managed to reach one of the books. "John Grisham," I read. "Who gives a shit?" I tossed it off the bookcase and reached the next book. "Stephen King. He can kiss my ass." I was down to the last three books, and I was losing hope. I couldn't reach them, no matter how I stretched, so I stepped onto one of the bookshelves and pulled myself up. Bracing my elbows on the top of the bookcase, I looked over the top. I couldn't make out what the last three books were. I needed to get closer.

I stretched out one hand toward the books and lost my balance, my left foot slipping off the shelf. Just before I fell to my death, I caught myself and got my foot back on the shelf. I took a deep breath and tried to calm myself while clutching onto the top of the bookshelf. Wow, being a reader took a lot of commitment.

My hand was hurting, and I noticed that it was bleeding. I must have cut it during my almost-fall. My stomach roiled, and I willed myself not to vomit. I couldn't stand blood. Any blood. Or violence. Or horror movies. In fact, I couldn't even handle bruised fruit. I was hyper sympathetic—or just a wimp. The actual diagnosis was up in the air. But the end result was that the drops of blood on the side of my thumb were making me dizzy and lightheaded. I looked down. It would be painful if I passed out and fell off the bookcase.

"Keep it together, Gladie," I told myself. "Stop being a wimp. Shut up. I'm wimp, and you'll have to deal with it." It was hard arguing with myself because I was really stubborn. But while I was battling my own neuroses, my thumb stopped bleeding, and the bookstore stopped spinning around.

After recovering, I grabbed two of the books. It turned out that they were the first two Harriet Hard books. My pulse raced, and my heart pounded in my chest. So close. So close. I tossed the two books onto the floor and squinted at the third book.

Hard to Die.

Bingo.

I found the book. I was three inches away from finding out if Harriet Hard survived, and if she took revenge on her arch-nemesis turned lover turned arch nemesis, Hugo Rockchenko. I couldn't wait!

All my hard work had paid off. I gave a cry of victory, shrieking in joy. The noise echoed in the empty store. I couldn't wait to get home with the book and get back into the Harriet Hard world. I stretched out my hand. My fingertips touched the spine of the book. I almost got it. I stretched further, and then finally, the book was in my hand.

And then it wasn't.

As I grabbed the book, I lost my balance. I swung my arm wildly, trying not to fall. The book flew from my hand and hit a wall before falling to the floor. My feet slipped, and I grabbed onto the top of the bookcase, hanging precariously in place. But the bookcase wasn't staying in place. With all of my movement, I had thrown the bookcase off balance, too. It rocked from side to side, spilling the books out onto the floor.

"This is going to be bad," I said.

The bookcase rocked until it couldn't rock anymore, and fell, taking me with it. The bookcase knocked into the next one, slamming me against the books. I slid down the other bookcase and fell to the floor. Luckily, the fallen paperbacks broke my fall.

"I survived," I said, surprised. I checked my body for broken bones, but I was fully intact. It was a miracle. I looked up to thank heaven for surviving. That's when I saw the rest of the books succumb to gravity and begin to rain down on me.

My first thought as the paperbacks hit my head was that critics called romance and mystery "light reading," but it sure felt heavy as it knocked me into unconsciousness.

CHAPTER 4

My eyes opened slowly. My head hurt, but it wasn't worse than the time a grenade went off in my bathroom while I was taking a shower. It would take more than a grenade to kill Harriet Hard, and if a grenade wouldn't kill me, I would definitely survive this.

Whatever this was.

Somehow I had been buried under a tower of books. I must have walked into the bookstore, looking for some research on weapons of mass destruction when my arch-nemesis Hugo Rockchenko attacked me and left me for dead.

"Not this time, Rockchenko!" I yelled, lifting my fist over my head.

I must have been getting close to zeroing in on his criminal enterprises, and so he decided to get aggressive. But it wouldn't dissuade me. I was going to shut down his nefarious activities, and make sure that he was brought to justice.

"Justice!" I announced and clutched my forehead. I was tough, but a couple of Advil would have come in handy while I worked for truth, justice, and the American Way.

I tossed aside the books that were on top of me and left the bookstore. As I reached the street, a car drove in my direction. I jumped in front of it and waved my hands. It screeched to a stop in front of me. I approached the driver's window and tapped on it. He opened.

"I'm an agent of a secret government agency," I told him. "I need your car. The lives of everyone in this country and a bunch of other countries depend on it."

"Are you fucking crazy?" the man demanded.

I put my head back and guffawed, loudly. "I wish," I said, seriously. "Being crazy would be a lot less stressful than trying to save the world. Open up and take me downtown. Now."

He unlocked the car, and I slipped into the passenger seat. "Burn rubber," I insisted. "Your country is depending on you."

We arrived at the Italian restaurant in fifteen minutes, and I thanked my driver. I walked inside. "A den of iniquity and infamy and other 'I' words," I announced loudly in the restaurant. It was late, and there were only a couple of diners left. "Don't think I don't know what is or isn't happening here."

"Hey, how are you Gladie?"

It was Jordan, the young, attractive man who was completely ignorant of the evil deeds around him. Oh, sweet, innocent, naïve man. But innocence never lasted long, and I knew that Jordan was going to be initiated in the world of international intrigue and villainy. It was just a matter of time.

I took his hand and pulled him aside. "Jordan, this is important. Rockchenko found me. We don't have a lot of time. There's a rat here, somewhere."

"Rat? We have an A-rating. Gladie, are you okay? Your head is bleeding."

"I don't care about blood, Jordan. I laugh at blood. And you might as well call me by my real name. I'm Harriet Hard, spy catcher."

He ran his fingers through his hair. "Huh?"

A man dressed as a chef ducked his head out of the kitchen and locked eyes with me. I squinted at him. He looked familiar, but I couldn't place him. Though he seemed to recognize me, and I scared him. He quickly averted his eyes and ran back into the kitchen.

I gripped Jordan's shoulders. "It's time to be brave, Jordan. Are you ready to help me in this battle against Rockchenko?"

"Gladie," he started.

"I told you, I'm Hard. Harriet Hard."

"Ms. Hard. I mean, Harriet. Harriet? Okay, Harriet. You see, Harriet, I think you might have gotten some bad medical marijuana. Or maybe one too many martinis?"

Jordan was good-looking, but he wasn't particularly bright. "I can assure you that I'm sharp as a tack, Jordan. As a tack. Besides, I have an almost inhuman ability to handle alcohol, illicit drugs, and Adam Sandler movies. Now, stiffen your spine and get ready. There might be bullets. Do yourself a favor and stick a frying pan in front of your face as soon as you can."

I took his large, manly hand and pulled him into the kitchen. I handed Jordan a frying pan and faced the chef who had hid from me. "Who sent you?" I demanded, sticking my finger under his nose. He had a large nose, as if a prawn was trying to eat his face.

"Who sent *you*?" he asked, shaking. Scared. Jackpot. There was nothing better than an operative way down the totem pole to get intelligence. And this guy was way down the totem pole from the looks of him. The bottom of the totem pole.

"I know everything," I told him, watching sweat roll down his face, like he had just run the hundred-yard dash in three seconds. "Everything. You've fallen in with a bad group. Evil. If you don't surrender yourself immediately, I can assure you that you'll wind up in a Supermax prison. Or worse."

"Worse?" he breathed, touching his throat. "But they'll kill me if I talk. Kill me!"

"I'm so confused," Jordan said.

The chef moved quickly. He was a ninja in a white chef's jacket. I had made the unforgivable sin of underestimating him,

50

and now I was going to pay the price for it. In a whir, he grabbed a long knife from the counter and waved it at me. With my lightning-fast reflexes, I jumped back in the nick of time.

"Jordan, the frying pan!" I yelled. Jordan threw the pan at the chef, managing to knock the knife out of his hand. I jumped at him, ready to subdue him with my judo, but he was wiry for a chef, and fast. He zipped out the back door before I could catch him. I started to run after him, but he was like the wind, blowing ahead of me and impossible to catch. So, I stopped, and with my sharp senses, I noticed the chef had dropped a scrap of paper. I picked it up and read it.

"Bruno Dominguez. Malibu." I tapped the paper against my chin, thinking. "Bruno Dominguez could be anybody. I need to get the agency's top cryptologists to figure this one out."

"Bruno Dominguez, the drug lord?" Jordan asked. His face was red and sweaty, like he was going to have a stroke. Since the rest of the kitchen staff had run for their lives, I got a glass and filled it with water for him. He took a sip. "They say Bruno Dominguez has killed ten thousand people. That's a lot of people, Gladie. I mean, Harriet."

"Not so many," I said, studying my nails. They were a mess, as if they hadn't seen a manicure in weeks, which was impossible because I had a weekly spa day that I never missed. Spy catchers have to look their best.

"They say he lives in a fortress in Malibu," Jordan explained, his voice strained. "It's a huge compound. His goons strong-armed Barbra Streisand and Suzanne Somers into giving up their properties so he could enlarge his compound. I hear that he has mutant, killer dogs that roam the property and eat trespassers, and that's the best way to go, because if Dominguez finds a trespasser, he kills them by removing body parts until they finally die."

I smiled. "Sounds perfect. We'll go just as soon as I get dressed."

I marched through the empty restaurant and climbed the stairs to the upstairs apartment with Jordan close on my heels. "Maybe we should call the police. Or maybe a doctor," he said.

"I told you, I'm fine."

"I meant for me. I don't know what's happening. One minute I'm Jordan, waiter and accounting student. And the next minute, I'm fending off knife-wielding chefs with ties to the most infamous drug lord on the planet."

"Oh," I said, waving my hand at him dismissively. "That's Tuesday for me." I tried the door of the apartment I had been using. "It's locked. Open it for me."

"I don't have the key."

I didn't have the key, either. I didn't have any belongings, it seemed. Obviously, the dastardly Rockchenko had stolen them.

"Break the door down," I told Jordan.

"Excuse me?"

I pointed at the door. "Give it a little shoulder action. The door is ancient. Balsa wood. It won't take much muscle," I said, eyeing his long, lean body. I was used to working with bulkier men than Jordan. Killers. Juice heads with serious knife skills.

Jordan crossed his arms in front of him. "Hey, I don't have a lot of time to work out, you know."

"Door."

"When I'm not working, I'm taking accounting classes. I'm buff for an accountant."

"Door."

"Have you ever seen an accountant with these guns?" he asked, flexing his biceps.

I put my hand on his shoulder. "Jordan, if you don't break down the door, I'm going to fashion a bomb out of Liquid Plumber and foie gras, and blow it all to shit. You get me?"

Jordan flinched. "I get you."

He took a deep breath and knocked into the door with his shoulder. The door gave way. "It worked," Jordan said, surprised. "How about that for muscles?"

I marched inside.

"Where's my Versace collection?" I asked, throwing ugly clothes out of the closet. "I know I'm undercover, but this is ridiculous."

"You always looked nice to me," Jordan said.

"Well, I'm gorgeous, sophisticated, and worldly, so of course you would think that. Luckily, I can pull off a Target t-shirt, but I shouldn't have to."

I ripped off my clothes and tossed them on the floor. I tossed a t-shirt to Jordan. "Put this on."

He put it up against his body. "It's too small."

"Exactly. You need to look the part." I put on a red bra and a skirt, which I ripped so that it showed as much leg as possible. "Give me your phone."

Jordan struggled to get the small shirt over his torso. "I don't understand what we're doing, and why I'm doing it with you."

"It's better to keep you in the dark," I said, digging his phone out of his pocket while he battled the t-shirt. "You'll probably die anyway, but the less you know, the more likely you'll die fast instead of being hanged by your thumbs until dead. Whoa, thumb-hanging is a bad death. It takes days."

Jordan inspected his thumbs. "They do that? That's possible? I don't want to die like that."

I pushed buttons on his phone, going online. "Ready? Let's go. It's destiny time."

Jordan put his foot down about driving to Malibu. He said

something about wanting to keep his thumbs. I had never worked with such a coward, but fearing death was common...or so I had heard. I had no fears, except for the fear of letting my country down. So, when Jordan refused to drive us in his Dodge Geo to the drug lord's fortress, I hogtied him with his lanyard, stuffed him into the back seat, and took the helm.

It was a beautiful evening in the City of Angels. Little did the citizens of Los Angeles know that there was evil in their midst. An evil that would stop at nothing to destroy civilization as we knew it. Luckily for them, Harriet Hard was on the case and would stop at nothing at stopping the evil from stopping at nothing.

I zipped around the traffic, using every ounce of my training in tactical driving. Time was of the essence when fighting a cartel of chaos commandos.

"I think the lanyard is cutting off the circulation in my legs," Jordan complained from the backseat.

"Don't worry. It won't permanently destroy your blood flow for another twenty-two minutes, and we'll get to Dominguez's house in no more than nineteen minutes."

Jordan whimpered. "I'm not sure I'm ready for my destiny. I'm an accountant."

I guffawed. "I think we both know that you're not an accountant, Jordan."

"I'm not?"

"Nope. At worst, you're a chef. At best, you're my new

sidekick."

"I'm afraid to ask you what happened to your old sidekick."

I turned the lights off as we approached the compound. I parked away from the surveillance and opened the back seat. "I'm going to untie you, now," I told Jordan. "I don't want you to run or scream. Your country needs you tonight, Jordan. Do you understand me?"

"I think so?" he said like a question.

I began to untie him. "We're going inside, and I'm going to interrogate Bruno Dominguez and force him to tell us where Hugo Rockchenko is before he kills us. Got it?"

Jordan was sweating, again. "What if Dominguez kills us?"

I ruffled Jordan's hair. "Funny one. A punk like Dominguez isn't going to get the drop on Harriet Hard."

"How are we going to get in? Do you have a rocket launcher or something?"

I gave Jordan my hand and helped him out of the car. "We're going to walk in through the front door. They won't notice us."

"Can you make us invisible? You're practically naked, and I'm wearing a shirt that's six sizes too small for me. I think we're pretty conspicuous."

"Not tonight we aren't. I put an ad on Craigslist with this

address on it, and the compound is about to get invaded by about three hundred people, give or take fifty people."

"An ad? What did you offer? Free cocaine?"

I nodded, thrilled that Jordan was starting to catch on. "Yep. Free cocaine and a free orgy. And I put ORGY in all caps. Come on, it's starting to get busy. See the crowd?"

We looked the part. I adjusted my breasts in my red bra and added more of a swing in my hips. Every inch of Jordan's torso was on display in my small shirt. We slid into the massive wave of orgy and cocaine seekers who were dressed in a similar level of skank. We were walking in a sea of leather, lace, and STDs. It was like a concert or an invasion. Dominguez's security made the mistake of letting the gate open a little, and the wave of humanity opened it the rest of the way. Then, there was no stopping them.

I noticed at least eight highly-armed security men, but since they couldn't shoot three hundred people, they were powerless. My plan was working.

"Get ready," I told Jordan.

"How? How do I get ready?"

"Don't open your mouth unless you're forced to, and in that case, lie. And run. Run real fast. And when you run, run low so you don't get shot."

Jordan wiped sweat off his forehead. "That's how I get ready? That's it? Oh my God. I don't like any part of that plan."

"Everyone's a critic." We got up the driveway without

incident and made it all the way to the front door, which had been opened by the force of the surge of people. "All right here we go."

CHAPTER 5

"Holy shit," Jordan said, as we were swept up into the house in the sea of orgy-seekers. It didn't take long for them to match up into partners, take their clothes off, and hop onto all available furniture, where they rutted like animals in heat. Dominguez's goons tried to break it up, but there was way too much sex happening to stop it. It was the perfect distraction for our mission.

"We have to find Dominguez before his goons gets this chaos under control," I told Jordan.

"We'll probably get herpes before we find him," Jordan commented, cutting a wide swath around a couple doing it doggie-style. "If my fiancée ever finds out that I was here, she'll kill me."

"Your fiancée. Yeah, right. You're never going to marry that woman. That's like taking poison, and you strike me as someone who wants to survive."

Jordan tripped over a naked man, but he caught himself before he fell on him. "What do you mean?"

I didn't have time to help Jordan out with his love life. In my experience, love sucked balls and warped good instincts. And generally made a person stupid. And crazy. Jordan would have to figure it out on his own. If it didn't affect our mission, I wanted nothing to do with it.

We walked past most of the orgy, and I stopped to get my bearings. The mansion was immense, and Dominguez could be anywhere. But evil was a funny thing. It acted like pretty much everyone in many ways. So, I would have bet my life—and I was always betting my life—that I would find him in the kitchen.

Jordan disagreed. "A guy like this has a man cave. You know, filled with electronics and massage chairs. We have to find his man cave."

I grabbed Jordan's hand and tugged him to the left, where I assumed the kitchen was. "A guy like this lives with his mother, and I bet right now she's cooking up a storm, while he's shielding her from seeing the tits and dongs in his living room."

I was right.

Of course.

We found the drug lord in a two story-high, cavernous kitchen of stainless steel and marble. His mother was at the stove, stirring several pots, and the smell was delicious, but since I rarely ate, I wasn't distracted. Instead, I gave my attention to Bruno Dominguez with my laser-sharp focus, honed over years of experience in the field.

"Get out, you freaks," he shouted, as Jordan and I entered the kitchen. He pulled out a large gun and waved it at us menacingly. I laughed and took a seat at the counter near his mother.

"Put it away, Bruno. You know that I could disarm you before you get a shot off."

"We're not freaks," said Jordan. "We're…well…"

"He knows who I am," I explained to Jordan. "Everyone in the underworld knows Harriet Hard, spy catcher. I eat men like him for lunch. For lunch."

Dominguez waved his gun, again. His face was brutal, a representation of all of the evil deeds he had committed in his life. A jagged scar trailed from the right side of his mouth, making him look like he was scowling permanently. He was a monster in a five-thousand-dollar suit. A brutal criminal who thought he was above the law.

I had news for him. He was about to meet justice. And her name was Hard. Harriet Hard.

"What the hell do you want?" he demanded.

"Is this how you're going to play this?" I asked. "Rockchenko. Hugo Rockchenko. Your boss. You're going to tell me where he is."

"My boss?" he asked, continuing to wave the gun.

"Or we could just go on our way," Jordan suggested.

"The chances of that are getting slimmer," Dominguez growled.

A couple goons ran into the kitchen. "Boss, it's all going to hell. It's like a giant porno movie, and now the cops are on their way."

Dominguez never lowered the gun. His aim was right for my head. Smart man. Nothing less than a bullet in my brain would stop me.

"Get the boys. Forget the naked people. Focus on putting you-know-what under wraps. I'll deal with the cops when they come," Dominguez ordered. He was a man who was used to being obeyed, and this time was no different. The goons hopped to it. The sound of moaning and men reaching climax reached us in the kitchen.

"I can't focus on my sauce," Dominguez's mother complained touching her face.

"I'll help you," Jordan said and shot a worried look at Dominguez and his gun. "Is that okay?"

"Do you know sauce?" his mother asked Jordan.

"He's a chef," I said.

She handed him a wooden spoon. "Stir quickly before Junior shoots you."

"Mama," Dominguez started.

"Oh, please, son. You and I both know these two are going to join the others in the pantry."

"What does that mean?" Jordan, asked, stirring a pot and sweating, again. "That sounds bad. I mean normally I like pantries, but I'm getting a bad feeling."

"We're getting off track," I interrupted. "If you don't cough up the GPS on your boss, Dominguez, I'm going to rearrange your face, and I'm going to start by moving your nose to your neck. You get me?"

"No," Dominguez answered. "But I get this. Nobody comes into my home and tells me what to do. So, I'm going to cut you into pieces and throw you outside to the animals protecting the border wall."

"That doesn't sound good either, Harriet," Jordan said, adding spices to the sauce. "None of that sounded good. Let's leave now before any of that starts. Okay? Okay? Please."

"None of that's going to happen," I told him, never taking my eyes off Dominguez. I was planning my attack. I was going to use my karate training to take his gun away and subdue him, completely. Then, I was going to move him to a small room and harshly interrogate him until he would give up the 411 on Rockchenko. I hopped off the stool and got into position, ready to pounce.

Then, four goons walked into the kitchen.

"We ditched the Sig Sauer's in the regular place, and the other stuff is taken care of," one of the goons said and then looked at Dominguez's gun. "The cops are here, boss. They're coming in now."

"What did you do to the sauce?" Dominguez's mother asked Jordan as she took a taste of it with a spoon. "It's the best sauce I've ever tasted."

Dominguez gestured with the gun to Jordan. "Get in the pantry."

Jordan dropped his spoon into the sauce, and his eyes got big. "The pantry? Not the pantry. Anything but the pantry."

"Grab the pussy and the chick," Dominguez ordered.

The goons picked up Jordan and walked him to the back of the kitchen. Two other goons went for me, and I got my karate chop hand ready, but they rushed me too fast. Overtaking my lightning reflexes and martial arts prowess, one of them lifted me over his shoulder and a couple of seconds later dumped me into the pantry on top of an open crate.

"Shut up while the cops are here," the goon warned Jordan and me. "Otherwise, the boss will kill you, the cops, and all of the freaks doing the nasty in the living room. Are you understanding my English?"

"I'm understanding your English," Jordan said. "Harriet, are you understanding his English? Please tell me that you're understanding his English."

"Fine. I'm understanding your English. For now. But after the cops leave, I'm going to kill you," I said.

They closed the door of the pantry. The room was filled with produce, cans, and dried meats. Luckily, the door was thin, because we could hear everything going on in the kitchen. A few seconds after we were locked in the pantry, the cops arrived.

"Look through the keyhole," I told Jordan from my seat, wedged in the crate. "Tell me what's happening."

He kneeled down and looked through the small hole. "There's a tall man in an Armani suit," he whispered to me. "He's surrounded by cops. Maybe we could escape now."

"Only if you want a bloodbath," I said. "Don't worry. I'll get you out of here no problem. When you're with me, you're bullet proof."

Jordan whimpered. "The Armani guy is up in Dominguez's face."

"Hello, detective," I heard Dominguez say.

"Are you kidding me?" another man said, his voice deep and annoyed. It was the detective. I recognized his voice of authority. "Have you moved on from drugs and contract killing to wild sex parties?"

"I think it was a practical joke," I heard Dominguez say.

"An ad was placed in Craigslist," the detective said and then started to laugh. "Sorry. Sorry," he said after a while. "An ad in Craigslist for an orgy at Bruno Dominguez's house!" He starting laughing again, hysterically. It was ballsy to laugh in Dominguez's face, but whoever it was laughing wasn't scared at all.

"The metrosexual detective is laughing in Dominguez's face," Jordan whispered. "He's going to get killed. Everyone's crazy today."

"I got to see this guy," I whispered, struggling to get out of the crate. Normally, I would have been able to hop out with no problem, but I was wedged in.

"He's got good hair," Jordan explained. "Tall. Armani suit with biker boots."

"What a time to choose to leave town," I heard the detective say. "I'm moving to the mountains, but I wouldn't mind taking down a drug lord before I go."

"What does that mean? Move to the mountains?" I asked myself, out loud. I finally rolled out of the crate and looked down at what I had been sitting on. "This is interesting," I muttered.

"The Armani detective's leaving the room. There's a lot of movement with the cops," Jordan told me.

I could hear the sound of the orgy participants being ushered out of the mansion. I didn't have a lot of time to finalize my plan.

"They're leaving," Jordan whispered. "Oh, dear God, the police are leaving. We're so going to die."

"We're not going to die," I said, picking up the crate.

"I'm not stupid. Nobody's really bullet proof, Harriet."

"I am," I told him, heaving the crate up.

Jordan stood up. "The detective's gone. I feel like my life is ticking away. Like this is Times Square, and it's New Year's and Anderson Cooper is counting down to me being shot full of holes." He stopped talking and looked at what I was holding. "What the hell is that?"

"A crate full of heads. Why? What does it look like?"

"Like a crate full of heads," he said and projectile vomited over the shelves of produce. The small room now smelled of half-digested pasta. Jordan wiped his mouth on his arm and took in deep breaths. "What are you doing with heads? Don't they freak you out?"

"Believe me, I've seen a lot worse than a crate full of heads. And there's no more than fifteen heads here. I've seen a lot more than that."

"Wow, you've got a terrible job," Jordan said.

"That's a laugh," I said. "You're going to be an accountant. I'd rather deal with severed heads twenty-four seven than earned income credits. And the worst thing is that you don't like earned income credits any more than I do, but you're going to do that because your pointy girlfriend's making you. I know that you'd rather be stirring sauce for the rest of your life. Do you hear that?"

"What?"

"Exactly. It's quiet. Get behind me. The plan still goes. We get Dominguez alone and find out where Rockchenko is. Remember that the future security of our country depends on it."

The door opened. A goon waved a gun at us. "Everyone out," he ordered.

I shook the crate of heads at him, and two of them flew out. Jordan wasn't the only one who was squeamish about severed heads. The goon shrieked like a little girl and jumped back, waving his hands wildly in order to fend off the heads. Thank God for squeamish men, because he was so scared that he dropped his gun.

"Pick it up, Jordan!" I yelled. I didn't turn around to see if he did what I told him. I ran at the other goons, tossing heads at them. Obviously, having severed body parts thrown at them wasn't part of their training because they ducked away. By the time I got near Dominguez, I had depleted the crate of heads.

And I had been wrong. There were actually twenty heads. It was quite a collection.

They did the trick. The goons parted like the Red Sea, and Jordan and I had a clear path to Dominguez. I ran at him like a bull charging a matador. With my lightning-fast reflexes and Olympic-quality judo techniques, I had no doubt I could take him.

Then, he pulled out a gun.

"Gun! Gun! Gun!" Jordan yelled, but it was unclear if he was talking about Dominguez's gun or the one Jordan had picked up because that's when the shooting began. Luckily, Dominguez was a terrible shot, so the bullets flew everywhere except right at me. Meanwhile, Jordan let rip with a volley of bullets himself. They went everywhere, too. The ceiling, the floor, the Keurig machine. Pretty much every appliance was shot full of holes. But I was fine.

Not a scratch anywhere on me. I wasn't surprised. I kept running for Dominguez. I was almost on him. My plan was almost done.

Unfortunately, however, the pot of sauce had been a victim of the shooting, and sauce had spilled all over the floor. As I ran at Dominguez, my foot stepped in a puddle of oily sauce, and I slipped. I sailed through the air, waving my arms in an effort to catch my balance. But no matter how incredibly coordinated I was, I was no match for an olive oil-doused red sauce.

I slammed into the marble counter, head first. The last thing I remembered before I lost consciousness was the sound of the marble cracking.

Or maybe that was my head.

My head hurt. It was probably a caffeine headache, and I just needed a cup of coffee. That happened occasionally when I slept too long. Oh, crap. The alarm must not have gone off, and I was going to be late for work at the bookstore.

The bookstore.

The bookstore.

Holy crap.

Memories flooded back to me. The bookstore. The Harriet Hard book. The accident. My head. And then believing I was Harriet Hard.

And the heads.

"Harriet, are you okay?"

I opened an eye. "Where am I?"

"Thank goodness you're alive." It was Jordan, and he was sitting on the floor, facing me. I was slumped on my side.

"I can't move my arms," I said.

"They zip-tied our wrists," he said, showing me his wrists.

"Who did?" I asked and then it all came back to me. "I touched a crate of heads, Jordan. I threatened a drug lord. I placed a Craigslist ad for an orgy."

"I know. I was there. Can you karate chop your way out of the zip ties? Do you have a plan for us to escape, Harriet?"

"I'm not Harriet. I'm Gladie," I said, breaking down into sobs.

"Are you going undercover again? Is that part of the escape plan? 'Cause we don't have a lot of time. They were just waiting for you to regain consciousness before they killed us. They said something about wanting to hear you scream. I guess unconscious people don't scream. But I'm pretty sure I would scream no matter what. So, what are you going to do? Blow something up? Judo? Call in the Navy Seals?"

All of that sounded real good. If only we could get someone to do any of that.

"Jordan, I'm not Harriet the spy catcher. I'm Gladie the temp. Some books fell on my head, and that's why I thought I was Harriet Hard. I guess I got my memory back when I knocked into the kitchen counter. I can't do judo or escape or anything. I pass out at the sight of blood."

"Are you making a joke?" Jordan asked, the sweat popping out on his forehead again. "I'm not good with humor. I never understood the joke about the chicken crossing the road. Why is that funny? Why do people laugh? It's just a chicken, and he's crossing the road. I don't get it."

He had a point. "What does that have to do with anything? We're about to die. I don't want to die."

Jordan studied me. "So, you're not Harriet Hard?"

"Harriet Hard is a character in a book. I'm just Gladie."

Jordan pounded the floor with his zip-tied fists. "Who does this happen to? How is this possible? It's like I'm in the Twilight Zone of LSD bad-trip nightmares. You dressed me for an orgy. I stirred a drug lord's sauce. I'm tied up on the floor of a man cave in a criminal compound, waiting to be murdered by a bunch of guys with fifty-inch-around necks."

"When you put it that way, it sounds bad," I said.

Jordan scooted on the floor toward me. He raised his fists up.

"What are you doing?" I asked.

"I'm going to hit you in the head so that you turn into

Harriet Hard, again."

I struggled to sit up and scooted away from him as fast as I could, but he scooted after me, waving his tied wrists. "But what if you kill me, or I think I'm someone even wimpier than me afterward?"

"I don't think that's possible."

"It's possible! There are people who are wimpier than me. Lots of them." It was a total lie. I was the gold-medalist of wimpiness. I was the Nobel Prize of wimpiness. After watching *The Wizard of Oz*, I had nightmares for a week, and that was just last month. It took three nurses to hold me down to give me a flu shot. I was the wimp of wimpdom.

"We need Harriet Hard and quick," Jordan said, his fists getting close to my head. "She would know how to get out of here. She would save us from the thumb-hanging."

"Thumb hanging? That doesn't sound good," I whined, scooting away from him.

"We need Harriet now. We have to escape. I'm going to punch you in the head to get her back. It won't hurt. I promise."

Jordan was a nice guy, and he didn't seem like a liar, but I was reasonably certain that getting punched in the head would hurt. "I don't think it works that way. I've gotten a lot of bumps on my head in the past, but this was the first time I turned into Harriet Hard."

"Maybe you're psychotic or something," he said scooting

toward me with his fists in position. "Maybe you're Sybil, and you have multiple personalities. Bring out the Harriet personality! Don't stick me with the wimp! I don't want to die!"

"I don't want to die, either. And getting punched in the head could kill me. I'm not Sybil. The Harriet Hard thing was a one-shot deal, Jordan. I promise."

But I wasn't sure about what I was saying. I had hit my head, and I had turned into Harriet Hard. Then, I hit my head, again, and I turned back into me. Maybe Jordan had a point.

He let his arms drop. "Okay. So, we're going to die. My head is going to be in the pantry, next to the persimmons, and the rest of me will be fed to the mutant killer dogs that guard the property."

That didn't sound good. "Maybe we can reason with them," I said. "Explain the whole Harriet Hard thing to them."

"They don't strike me as the reasonable type. You went on and on about his boss. I don't think he liked that. Holy shit. Do you hear that?"

I heard it. Dominguez was coming with his goons, and they were talking about the details of our torture and murder. "Jordan, I don't want my head to wind up in a crate in the pantry," I whined.

"Be Harriet Hard. Please," he said.

I closed my eyes and wished that I was Harriet Hard, but when I opened them again, I was still Gladie Burger.

But I wanted to survive.

I looked around the room. It was the man cave of an incredibly rich man. There were plenty of electronics, but no weapons.

But there were floor-to-ceiling windows. "Help me up," I told Jordan.

Luckily, our wrists were zip-tied in front of our bodies instead of behind our backs. We tried the windows, but they were all locked. "The end table looks heavy," I said. Without another word, as if we could read each other's minds, we grabbed either side of the table and hurled it through the window. The sound was deafening. We didn't look back when we jumped through the broken window, which was a good thing because the door to the man cave opened the moment the glass broke, and I didn't want to see our killers come after us.

We fell about ten feet to the ground below. My high heels snapped in two on impact, but somehow, I stayed upright and started running away from the mansion.

"We are so going to die," I cried. The compound was huge, situated on acres of land, but it didn't take long to see the wall that marked the boundary of the property. We ran faster toward it.

"They're chasing us!" Jordan yelled.

It was harder than I expected to run with my hands tied and my heels broken, but it was amazing how my survival instincts kicked in and gave me cardio superpowers. We got near to the wall when we saw the mutant killer watch dogs coming straight for us.

"Dogs!" I shouted as a warning to Jordan.

"Not dogs. Men. They're standing up."

I squinted. It was the middle of the night, but with the lights from the house and the moon above, I could make out the figures. They were tall and hairy, like dogs on their hind legs. And hopping.

Hopping, stand-up, mutant killer attack dogs.

"They're hopping, stand-up dogs," I announced to Jordan.

"What's a hopping, stand-up dog?"

We didn't have long to wait to find out. They were coming right for us, and we were going right for them. It was either that or turn around onto the path of the goons who were chasing us with their guns.

We were stuck between a rock and a hard place. Between goons with guns and hopping, stand-up mutant attack dogs.

"If I get out of this alive, I'm never going to read another book ever again!" I shouted and kept running.

Hop, hop, hop, the dogs came for us. Just as they were about ten feet away, I realized that they weren't dogs at all. Jordan figured it out at the same time.

"Kangaroos!" Jordan cried, relieved. "They're just kangaroos. The drug lord has some kind of freaky zoo. That's all.

Come on! Nobody's scared of a kangaroo. They're harmless."

Funny how irony invades a conversation. In my experience, "famous last words" should have been added to most statements. And this wasn't any different. No, nobody was scared of kangaroos. They had pockets in their bellies. They had cute noses. They hopped. They were from Australia. Why would anyone be scared of a kangaroo?

But we were about to find out that these weren't ordinary kangaroos. Dominguez had crazy, killer kangaroos.

The worst kind of kangaroos.

A couple went after Jordan, a couple went after me, and luckily, the rest went after the goons. They were equal opportunity, crazy, killer kangaroos. They didn't care who they attacked. I ducked and weaved, but no matter how awesome I was in spin classes, I was no match for a large marsupial. Neither was Jordan. The two kangaroos pounded him.

The goons ran for their lives back to the house. We were home free! We just had to avoid the kangaroos and make it over the wall to freedom. Easy peasy.

Ouch!

Sonofabitch!

One of the killer kangaroos made contact with my back. It was like it knew karate or kung fu. And it was strong. I flew forward a few steps but managed not to fall. Jordan was getting pounded. We were only a few feet from the wall. I ran to Jordan and tried to help him up. I grabbed his hand and pulled.

That's when one of the killer kangaroos caught me at the back of my head, and everything went dark.

Again.

Damn it.

Harriet Hard had had a long day. Saving the world was difficult, even for her. But now the world was saved, and it was time to go home. No, she wasn't going to her villa in Italy or her chalet in Switzerland. She wasn't in the mood for her brownstone in Manhattan or her plantation in Louisiana. She was going home to Grandma's house. Home. It was a Victorian house made of wood, but it was really made of heart and love.

She drove her Ferrari on the windy road that led up the mountains to the small town where her grandmother lived. She took the curves easily at a breakneck speed, her driving skills the envy of every race car driver in the world.

Harriet parked in her grandmother's driveway and got out of her car. Her grandmother opened the door to the house and stepped out.

"Dolly, I made up your room. There's fried

chicken in the kitchen waiting for you."

Harriet walked inside. "My arch-nemesis turned into my lover and back to my arch-nemesis," she told her grandmother. "I saved the world, but I'm not sure I saved myself."

Her grandmother put her hand on Harriet's cheek. "You have the gift, bubbeleh. Your place is here. You're home."

"But I have to travel the world and diffuse bombs."

"You have the gift. Your place is here. You're home. Home…home…home…"

"Gladie, you're not dead, are you?"

"I'm saving the world with fried chicken," I moaned and slowly became aware of my surroundings.

I was lying flat on my back on the sidewalk, and Jordan was leaning over me. A streetlight gave me a good look at his face, which was a picture of concern and a bruised, swollen eye.

"Are you Harriet, again?"

"I thought I was, but I guess I was dreaming," I said. The dream had been very real, and it left me with a lot of food for thought. It had been like my grandmother had really been talking to me. And she was inviting me home. I hadn't had a real home since I was a little girl, before my father died. But that had been a long time ago, and I had been running away and trying to return home at the same time, ever since.

Wow, there was nothing like being attacked by a killer kangaroo to have a life-changing insight.

"Where am I?" I asked Jordan.

"On the other side of the wall. The kangaroos got tired of karate chopping us and hopped away. I lifted you up over the wall. I haven't heard from Dominguez or his men. I guess they gave up on us."

Jordan helped me up. I checked my body for injuries, but somehow, I had made it out of the drug lord's den in one piece. We were still zip-tied, but Jordan said he had scissors in his car.

"How did you get me over the wall?"

"I told you that I'm buff for an accountant."

While I had been Harriet, I had hidden Jordan's keys behind the little door to the gas tank. We fished them out and opened the car. Jordan cut my ties, and I cut his. This time, he drove.

"I'm sorry about tonight. About everything," I told him, as we drove away from the fancy neighborhood.

"It wasn't your fault. You thought you were Harriet Hard."

"I'm never going to read a book again. Books are dangerous. They make you think you're someone you're not. They give you ideas. Dangerous ideas."

"I don't think it was the book's fault. I think your brain got confused."

I looked in the side-view mirror for any sign of Dominguez or his men, but it was the middle of the night and the roads were empty except for Jordan's car. It looked like we had gotten away scot free. Dominguez didn't strike me as the kind of guy who would let his would-be victims dangle in the wind with the possibility of them reporting about kidnapping and severed heads to the police.

"Why aren't they following us?" I asked Jordan.

"They don't know where we are. They don't know what car I have. They had gotten busy with the kangaroos, and now they're looking for Harriet Hard. Luckily, you're not Harriet Hard anymore. So, they'll never find us. We can go back to our normal lives."

I was surprised to realize that I was disappointed to go back to my normal life. My life wasn't anything resembling normal, but it wasn't anything resembling exciting or fulfilling, either. Becoming Harriet Hard was the first fun I had had since I could remember.

"That's good," I lied.

"Yeah, good," Jordan said, his voice drifting off.

"I mean, you're getting married, and you're going to be a CPA. A house in Brentwood. That should be nice."

"Bel Air," he corrected. "I guess that's good."

"Sure it is."

"I'll spend my life crunching numbers so that rich guys can evade paying taxes. Chained to a desk all day, every day, to come back to a house that's mortgaged to the hilt."

"To a woman you love," I added, putting a good spin on it.

"Yeah…love…" he said, his voice drifting off again.

Harriet Hard wasn't real, but she had left us a mirror to reflect our lives back to us. And what we saw wasn't good. I was doomed to return to one temp job after another, to one bad date to another. Never enough money to pay my meager bills. No goals, no missions, no hope.

But at least I didn't have a pointy woman bossing me around. That would have been the camel that broke my hairy back.

"I'll be working so hard that I'll never have time to make boeuf bourguignon or a soufflé. Those are very time-consuming meals to prepare," Jordan continued. He was deep in thought, and it seemed like he was talking to himself, not to me. "I'll never have time to learn to make good mole. Never. I was going to go down to Mexico to learn it from a hundred-and-five-year-old lady. Now, I'll be too busy figuring out deductions for business yacht trips to ever cook again."

Never cooking again sounded great to me. My cooking skills ended at toast and a half-decent cup of coffee. "Maybe she'll let you cook a soufflé once in a while," I said, trying to cheer him up.

Jordan barked a laugh. "Are you kidding? If she lets me make her a ham and cheese sandwich, I'll be lucky."

I didn't have a response to that. Jordan was in a bad place. He was doomed to accounting and a woman who wouldn't let him sauté. He couldn't find a way out.

It was a bad sign when you wished you were still zip-tied in a drug lord's compound, waiting to be dismembered.

I got three hours of sleep before I had to get up to go to work at the bookstore. Jordan and I had agreed to pretend the night hadn't happened and not to tell another living soul about Harriet Hard and Dominguez. Besides the restaurant's runaway cook, there were no real witnesses to my alter ego who also knew me as Gladie Burger.

So, we were going on as if nothing had happened.

I dressed in a skirt and a blouse and took the bus to the bookstore, since I couldn't find my keys or my purse. My boss Francine met me at the door.

"You!" she growled and stomped her foot. "You! You! You!"

It wasn't the first time a boss had had that reaction to me.

"Good morning, Francine. How are you?"

"You destroyed my shop! It's like a bomb went off in here. And you left the door unlocked."

"I what?" I asked, but the memories flooded back to me. The bookcases. The books. I pushed Francine aside and walked inside. I had to see the scene of the crime. The birthplace of Harriet Hard.

It was worse than I had imagined. Francine had been right. It looked like a bomb had gone off. All the bookcases except for the ones along the walls had fallen over. There were books everywhere, like someone had left the lid off of a book popcorn popper. My organization was shot to hell. Romance, mystery, and science fiction were all mixed together in no order whatsoever. All my hard work was ruined. I found my purse at the bottom of a pile, and I slipped it over my shoulder.

"I never should have hired you," Francine screeched. "I could tell you were no good, and it was obvious that you're not a reader."

"I've read two books this week!" I screeched back. It was the truth, but she was right. I had read two books, but I wasn't a reader. I didn't know anything about books.

But I knew what was going to happen next. It had happened a million times. I was going to get fired.

Sacked. Laid off. Axed. Canned.

"You're…" Francine started, while I looked at my nails. Her voice rose, and I knew she wanted to yell "fired" to really hit home the message.

It was a shame because I had enjoyed the job, and I had started to read. But never again. I was reasonably sure I had run out of decent jobs, and no way was I ever going to get involved with a book series again. Harriet Hard could go straight to hell, as far as I was concerned.

Francine didn't shout "fired," however, because she was interrupted. Several men walked into the small shop. A tall man entered first. He was well-dressed in a beautiful, gray suit and an overcoat, which was strange because it was a warm, Southern Californian day. He was blond and probably in his sixties, and he seemed extremely pleased to see me.

Behind him were two men, each about a head shorter than the first man and both dressed in baggy, black suits. One of them held tight to Jordan, one hand clenched around his arm, and the other hand holding a knife to his throat.

"Harriet Hard, I presume," the man in the overcoat said, looking at me.

CHAPTER 6

"What's going on here?" Francine demanded.

"I hear that you've been looking for me, Ms. Hard," the man in the overcoat said, ignoring Francine and looking right at me. I shuddered. He gave me the creeps. Jordan was staring at me, too. He was worried, and there was something else in his expression. Guilt that he had led them to me?

"May I help you? This is my establishment," Francine continued, valiantly trying to control the situation.

The man in the overcoat signaled one of the men, and he grabbed Francine's arm. "Don't hurt her," I urged.

The man looked at his boss, and the boss nodded. "Just make sure she won't cause any trouble."

"What does that mean?" Francine asked, panic invading her voice. They didn't answer her. The man lifted her up, tucked her away in the supply closet, and barred the door.

I had to think quick to get us out of the jam. And by jam, I meant getting murdered. I willed my brain to think like Harriet Hard or like anyone who was half-competent. But nothing came to me. My brain refused to cooperate. Instead of working out a strategy to survive, I only managed to drum up fear, anxiety, and dread.

"I'm not Harriet Hard," I told the man.

He shot a look at Jordan, and Jordan shrugged. "I hear that you've been looking for me," the man said.

"Dominguez's boss," I breathed. Somehow as Harriet Hard, I had stumbled on the truth about the so-called biggest drug lord on the planet: he had a boss.

"Drew Forest. Nice to meet you."

"He's the local assemblyman," Jordan squeaked.

Holy cow. It was a conspiracy with a drug lord and a politician. It was like a really good movie with bad guys and knives and killer kangaroos.

But as much as I loved those kinds of movies, I didn't want to live in one. It was scary, and I didn't do scary very well.

"I'm not Harriet Hard. Here's what happened. It's a funny story, actually. Harriet Hard is actually a character in a book that I was reading. Then, I got hit on the head and thought I was Harriet Hard. But I'm nothing like her. I'm a coward. And I don't care about crime. Crime is fine. And I'm not a snitch. I've never snitched. I'm snitchless." I smiled at him to show how harmless I was. He didn't look convinced. "And Jordan is a waiter, studying to be an accountant. You can't get more boring than that," I added for good measure.

"She's telling the truth," Jordan whined. "I'm a waiter, and she's a big loser. She used to clean cement trucks. She's a really big loser. The biggest loser in the world."

I pointed at Jordan. "Exactly. I'm a loser temp worker. I can't hold down a job. I don't know anything about drug lords and assemblymen. I don't even know what one does. What do you do? I mean, besides this?"

"I'm going to find out how you knew about me, when I've been the best kept secret since the Manhattan Project," he answered.

"What's the Manhattan Project?"

"No more jokes," he said, even though I wasn't joking. "Come on, gentlemen, let's get these two to the ice house. We'll freeze up the lines of communication before this gets out of hand."

"But I'm snitchless," I blubbered, as one of his men grabbed me from behind and started to push me out of the shop.

The long and varied history of torture played in my mind as Jordan and I were abducted. Bamboo under fingernails, sleep deprivation, beatings, a low carb diet. I wouldn't be able to handle any of that. But they didn't believe me about Harriet Hard. They didn't believe that I was a big loser.

Idiots.

I needed to figure out a story that I could tell to satisfy the assemblyman about how I knew Dominguez had a boss, and that I wasn't a threat and he should let Jordan and me go free. And not dead.

Think. Think. Think, I told myself, as they shoved us outside and walked us forcibly toward a black SUV. There was no mistaking by any casual observer that we were being abducted. But nobody walking by came to our rescue. Nobody called 911 for our benefit.

Geez, what had society come to? Where's a Boy Scout when you needed him? If things got any worse, I would have to start voting.

Then, Nat Pendleton got involved. Nat, the man who made my flesh crawl, violently shoved the man who was holding me out of the way.

"Listen, bitch," Nat yelled at me. "I thought about it all night. You owe me. You ate two entrees. Two! And all I got for it was electrocution and a bill from the ambulance company."

Blech. Nat was worse in daylight.

My abductor pushed Nat away from me. "Look, buddy," he started.

Like giving a jump to a car battery, my brain finally whirred into action. While Nat fought with the men, I signaled to Jordan, and we ran full out.

"Where are we going?" Jordan asked, as we ran down the block.

"Away!" I shouted back.

He took my hand and sped up. Thank goodness for spin classes so that I could keep up. This time there were no killer kangaroos, but there was no place to hide, either. I snuck a look behind us to see that Nat was holding his nose, and our three abductors were getting into their SUV.

"We have to find a hiding place!" I shouted.

We ducked into the building on the corner. A woman sat at the receptionist desk in the large lobby. "Welcome to Cannabis College," she said, smiling. "Are you here for the tour?"

"Cannabis College?" Jordan asked. "Is that a thing?"

I could hear the SUV screeched to a stop on the street outside. They had found us. "Yes," I told the receptionist. "We're here for the tour. Let's get going now."

She gave us two nametags shaped like marijuana leaves, and Jordan and I hastily scribbled our names on them and stuck them to our chests.

"Let's go. Let's go," Jordan urged her. "I need a tour of the Cannabis College."

"I love your enthusiasm," the woman said. "My name's Twilight, and I'll be your tour guide. Would you follow me?"

We followed her, half-pushing her out of the lobby and

into the building.

"Cannabis College was started in 2016 to educate those interested in cannabis or for those interested in getting into the business of helping people," she explained.

"Where did she go?" I heard the assemblyman say from down in the lobby. "Find her."

We walked upstairs in a hurry. "This is one of our classrooms," Twilight told us, opening a door.

"Good. Let's go in and see it," I said. Jordan and I jumped inside.

"Maybe we can shove the tables up against the door," Jordan said, looking around.

"I don't think that'll do it," I said. "Where does that door lead to?" I asked Twilight, pointing to a door in the corner.

"The laboratories. But tours are only allowed to look through the window in the hallway. There's no access for you. I'm sorry. Our laboratories are state of the art. Very scientific."

She was smiling ear-to-ear, and I hated to burst her bubble, but I could hear death marching toward us.

"Listen, Twilight," I said. "There're men out there who want to kill us, and I don't suggest that you get in between them and us. You know what I mean? You got to run away quick and let us know where we can hide."

Twilight's smile disappeared. "My mom told me this job

would be dangerous. Weed is the gentle drug? Yeah, right. My ass. I'm out of here. You're on your own."

She ducked out through the corner door, and we followed her. The laboratories were actually rows and rows of pot plants. Light shined down from the ceiling, which I assumed made them grow. It wasn't the perfect place to hide. We would have to find someplace else. I wanted to follow Twilight, but she was already long gone, darting between the pot plants and out of the room.

"Not so fast," the evil assemblyman roared as he entered the laboratory with his two henchmen. They had found us. "You're making me angry, Ms. Hard."

I stomped my foot on the floor. "I told you that I'm not Harriet Hard! She's not a real person!"

I searched for anything that could be used as a weapon, but there was nothing except for weed. Jordan thought faster. He ripped two plants out of the dirt and threw them at the bad guys. I did the same thing, but it had little effect.

"Hurry!" Jordan shouted and took my hand. We ran out of the laboratory and down the hall. Our pursuers were fast on our heels. It didn't look like we would ever escape, and then I heard a shot ring out and crash through a window near my head.

"Don't kill them here!" the assemblyman shouted. "We have to interrogate them first."

I hoped they listened to him. Jordan and I stopped at a dead end.

Tasting Room was written on the door. Jordan and I exchanged looks. We both shrugged at the same time, and he opened the door.

Inside was a large room. There were about a dozen people in it, sitting on chairs and the floor. At least I thought they were. I couldn't be sure because they were all smoking, and the room was filled with smoke, making visibility difficult.

"Uh oh," Jordan said, wheezing. "I have asthma."

"Hold your breath," I told him.

He took a deep breath and went into a coughing fit. "I'm dying," he wheezed. "And I'm high as a kite. What's this stuff made of?"

The door opened behind us, and the bad guys ran in. Jordan and I hid under a table.

"Oh, man. I can't take weed, man. It makes me crazy paranoid," one of the henchmen complained.

"So, get Harriet Hard and her sidekick on the double, and let's get out of here," the assemblyman ordered.

We could see their feet, as they shuffled around, inspecting the smokers to see if they were us. It was only a matter of time until we were discovered. Meanwhile, we were breathing in at least a half dozen strains of super-strength marijuana. I giggled, and Jordan threw his hand over my mouth, while he had a coughing fit.

"What's that! What's that!" the paranoid henchman yelled.

"The soldiers are after us! They're going to get us with their orange flying cars! The cars are shooting poison darts at us! Duck!"

As far as I could make out, the paranoid one jumped on his buddy, and they fell to the floor. "Watch out for poison darts!" he yelled and punched his friend in the face. His friend punched him back. They rolled along the floor, beating the hell out of each other.

Jordan lowered his hand from my mouth, and he gasped for air. "You want chips?" I asked him. "I could go for chips. And fried chicken. I would kill a puppy for chips. You think they have chips here? Maybe a snack machine? Do they sell guacamole in snack machines? Guacamole would go great with chips. And fried chicken. And bacon. And a chocolate cake. And Pop Tarts. Oh, Pop Tarts would be really good right now."

Jordan coughed. "I'm... going... to... die," he gasped. "Can't... breathe... must... stop... him." Crawling out from under the table, he grabbed the assemblyman's leg, making him fall to the floor. "You're... not... going... to... kill... me," Jordan gasped. He straddled him and raised his fist over his face. "I'm... not... going... to... die... from... from... from. Screw it."

Jordan gave up trying to talk and breathe. With every ounce of strength he could muster in his asthmatic, accountant body, he slammed his hammer fist onto the politician criminal's face.

Pow! One punch was all it took. He was out cold. Luckily, the other two were unconscious, too, victims of each other.

"Help... Gladie..." Jordan gasped.

I helped him out of the room. I sat him on the floor in the hallway where there was fresh air, and I leaned him up against the wall. Once I was sure that he could breathe again, I went back into the tasting room and enlisted the help of the potheads to tie up the three criminals with strong hemp rope.

"What strain did they smoke?" one of them asked me.

"A new one. It's in the laboratory. Third plant from the left. The very last row."

They filed out of the tasting room to find the holy grail marijuana plant that knocked men out cold. Finally, the room emptied of smoke and I could see clearly, even though I was still high as a kite.

The three bad guys roused, but they were hog-tied and couldn't move. "Nobody messes with Harriet Hard!" I yelled at them. "You're all going to jail now! Harriet Hard always gets her man!"

"I knew you were lying about not being Harriet Hard," the assemblyman sneered.

"You think they have chips here?" I asked.

"I saw a machine," the paranoid henchman told me.

"Where?" I asked.

"Downstairs. Behind Jesus."

The cops arrived while I was downstairs eating chips and Snickers bars. Since everything was in hand, I decided to take my junk food and walk home where my bed was waiting for me. Outside, there were at least ten cop cars, two ambulances, and three or four news crews. Nobody noticed me as I walked by, gnawing on a Snickers.

When I arrived home, I plopped down on the couch and turned on the television. After watching a commercial for toilet bowl cleaner, I fell into a deep sleep. A few hours later, I woke, sober with a slight stomachache. The news was on TV, and Jordan was the star. He was being interviewed, and I was surprised to see the pointy woman standing next to him. I was even more surprised to see my boss Francine standing behind them. She had gotten free.

"Then they went into the building, and I followed, and they went there and they went here and then they went back to there and here, again," he told a reporter, his pupils large black saucers. "Then, I hog-tied them and called the police. I believe in justice. And freedom. And, you know, other Superman things."

The reporter nodded. "How do you feel, revealing a criminal conspiracy in Los Angeles and taking down the world's largest drug cartel?"

"It feels pretty good," he said, seeming to think about it.

"And what are you going to do with your reward money?"

"The reward money?" he asked.

"Fifty thousand dollars," the reporter explained.

Jordan smiled and looked directly into the camera lens. "I'm going to start my own restaurant."

The pointy woman cleared her throat. "What he means is that he's going to finish school and start his accounting practice," she said.

Jordan turned toward her. "Nope. I'm opening a restaurant."

"But we're getting married."

"Are we?" Jordan asked, smiling.

The couple argued on live TV about what Jordan would do with his reward money. I would have liked some of it, but I was happy to see Jordan standing up for himself for the first time and following his dream.

My phone rang, and I answered it.

"Hello, Dolly." It was my grandmother. "I cleaned up your room, and the fried chicken will be here in an hour."

It was like my Harriet Hard dream was coming true. My room. My fried chicken. Sanctuary.

And boy, fried chicken sounded good. So did a nice room in my grandmother's house.

"But what will I do there?" I asked her.

"You have the gift, bubbeleh. You're going to be a matchmaker like your Grandma. You'll help me run the business."

"But I don't know how to be a matchmaker," I said.

"You have the gift. You'll see. Won't it be nice to live here and give people their happily ever afters?"

That did sound nice. But I didn't want to let my grandmother down, and I was supremely talented in letting employers down.

"You won't let me down," Grandma told me, somehow reading my mind. "I see you, Gladie. I see you. I know who you are, and I love you. And I know that you have the gift."

"I guess I could come for a couple months and see how I do," I said, warming to the idea, but unwilling to commit.

If I got in my car now, I could be at her house in a couple of hours. Safe. Loved. It was a mighty big temptation. Sure, I was scared and totally certain that I would be a terrible matchmaker, but my grandmother had a way of knowing things that couldn't be known, and maybe she knew this. Maybe I did have the gift.

"Okay," I said finally. "But no matchmaking directed at me. I'm through with men."

"I'll leave you in charge of matchmaking for yourself," Grandma said.

"Good, because I'm done with men. Finito. I'm never dating again."

"If you say so."

"It'll be nice to be somewhere calm where nothing happens," I told her, getting up from the couch. I dug my suitcase out from under my bed and started to pack. "You won't believe what happened to me in the past couple days. Mayhem! Severed heads! Luckily nothing like that ever happens in Cannes. Total calm. Peace. Serenity. Yep, maybe you're right, Grandma. It's time for me to settle down and relax. A nice quiet life. That's what I want."

"If you say so, bubbeleh," Grandma said.

And don't forget to sign up for the newsletter for new releases and special deals: http://www.elisesax.com/mailing-list.php

ABOUT THE AUTHOR

Elise Sax worked as a journalist for fifteen years, mostly in Paris, France. She took a detour from journalism and became a private investigator before writing her first novel. She lives in Southern California with her two sons.

She loves to hear from her readers. Don't hesitate to contact her at elisesax@gmail.com, and sign up for her newsletter at http://elisesax.com/mailing-list.php to get notifications of new releases and sales.

Elisesax.com
https://www.facebook.com/ei.sax.9
@theelisesax

Manton Public Library
404 West Main Box F
Manton, MI 49663-0906
(231) 824-3584

CADILLAC WEXFORD PUBLIC LIBRARY

33058308

Mystery **WEEDED**

Sax, Elise.

Road to matchmaker

√/19 matchmaker #0.5

CPSIA information can be obtained
at www.ICGtesting.com
Printed in the USA
FSHW01n0727300818
51883FS

9 781978 443297